heathrow nights

Jan Mark

Hodder
Children's
Books

A division of Hodder Headline Limited

First published in Great Britain in 2000
by Hodder Children's Books

A Catalogue record for this book is available from the British Library

ISBN 0 340 77411 8

Typeset by Avon Dataset Ltd, Bidford-on-Avon, Warks

Printed and bound in Great Britain by
The Guernsey Press Co. Ltd, Channel Isles

Hodder Children's Books
A division of Hodder Headline Limited
338 Euston Road
London NW1 3BH

For Simon Puttock

One

We intercepted the letters. I don't know if the others read theirs, I opened mine standing there in the hall, with the rest of the envelopes on the carpet, fanned out, face down, just as they had been when they landed. With a criminal instinct I didn't know I possessed I'd marked all their positions before I scooped them up, picked out mine and put them back again.

Only it wasn't mine.

I started to take it out of the envelope addressed to Mrs S. Jagger, with the school's name printed along the top, the school not having yet caught up with the fact that she is no longer Mrs S. Jagger but Mrs S. Hague. The school, in the person of head honcho McPherson, has a lot of catching up to do. If he'd wanted to avoid people like me doing what I was at that very moment doing, he should have used a plain envelope. If he had *really* thought about it he'd have used e-mail, but for all the stuff about IT in the prospectus, and the hardware cluttering up the place, bad news still goes out on paper and falls into the hands of promising crims: me, Curtis and Adam. Very bad news, all three of us.

Mr Hague and the new Mrs Hague were still in bed, it being Saturday, but Mum was sure to have heard the postman crashing about, so I didn't stop to read McPherson's letter, I just glanced at the first lines: *Dear Mrs Jagger, I regret to inform you that your son Russell* . . .

I knew the rest. McPherson had given it to us in very plain prose the previous morning.

Overhead the floorboards creaked. Mum was getting up, fairy-footed. Hague hits the mat like boots dropping from a great height. I slid the letter back into the envelope and tore it across, from top to bottom, the two halves into four, the four into eight. After that it wouldn't tear, but by then Mum was closing the bathroom door and I was in the kitchen, filling the kettle.

When she came downstairs I was ladling coffee into the cafetière, laying out biscuits. I heard her go along the hall to pick up the post; seven envelopes, a Jiffy bag and a magazine, shrink-wrapped to keep the germs out. *The* letter was not there, it never had been there, it did not exist. There were some scraps of paper in my back pocket, to be disposed of later. Can't imagine where they came from, it's amazing the junk that collects in back pockets.

Mum came into the kitchen, already sorting the mail into his'n'hers.

'Nothing for you, sorry.' There never is anything for me. Then she saw what I was doing. 'Coffee in bed? Oh, Russ, that's nice of you.'

She continued to believe that I continued to be nice, in the intervals of being a complete bastard. I saved the bastard for school, mainly. I had nothing against Hague – as a Hague, that is. Occasionally I even referred to him as Chris, which was what I called him to his face (as opposed to Dickhead at school for appearances' sake). In private he was Claudius, but that was a private joke between me and me. And if he'd known about it he wouldn't have understood anyway. As a stepfather he was irrelevant. He could have come the heavy, but from the point where marriage was on the cards he became very cautious and conciliatory. During a periodic search of his belongings I came across a book about being a step-parent. So he was *trying*. I'd have preferred it if he hadn't tried, which was one of the reasons the letter from McPherson had ceased to be. If he'd got wind of what was happening he'd have had to play parents, something he'd been avoiding for five months – except for reading about it.

'I'm not trying to replace your father,' he said to me urgently, once.

I said, 'You couldn't.'

'I know,' he said, humbly, which is why he'd said he wasn't trying to in the first place, I suppose, but I didn't see why I should give him an easy ride.

'I won't do anything unless it's all right with you,' he said, but he went right ahead and did it, even though he must have been able to see it wasn't all right, although he kept, well, almost deferring to me. I half expected him to corner me in private and say, 'Sir, I have come to ask for your mother's hand in marriage.'

Perhaps she had told him about Adam. Adam went right off the rails when his mother shacked up with the Beast from Bedford, and took his sisters with him like the string of little lady carriages behind Thomas the Tank Engine. As they were all at different schools it was quite a pile-up: teachers, social workers, psychologists and, at one point, doctors. And cops. Because I hadn't done an Adam I was suspected of bottling things up and everybody was getting ready to duck and run when I finally broke out.

And anyone who hangs with Adam gets caught in the searchlights, but it wasn't Adam who got us into this mess, it was Curt.

On the face of it, Curt has nothing to complain of. You could do a checklist; stable two-parent family, rich cultural background – rich background period – Christian family values. They are not Curt's values. Curt's values can be measured by the gram, he smokes anything that will ignite. Quite what he was on when they took us to *Hamlet* at the Theatre Royal is anyone's guess. He just sat and giggled to himself very quietly through the first half, when he wasn't asleep. Unfortunately he *was* asleep by Act III Scene 3, and woke up just as Hamlet was getting ready to stab his uncle Claudius – his stepfather – from behind. That was when they threw us out.

I've read it right through and seen two movie versions so I know how it ends, but Curt still hasn't found out what happens. In the theatre he was sitting at the end of the row, me on one side, Adam on the other, easy to get at, easy to eject, all three. Thrown out of the Theatre Royal.

'Great bloke, Hamlet,' Curt says, monotonously. 'Does he win?'

'Win what?'

'At the end; does he win?'

'No,' Adam says, 'he doesn't win.' Adam only knows this because I told him.

'What's the point of it all, then?' Curt says. Curt has not got his head around the concept of tragedy, the point of which is that the hero does not win. Which is why I wish I had never started calling Hague 'Claudius'.

Him Claudius. Me Hamlet.

You know what happens in *Hamlet*.

Maybe not. Young guy at Uni gets a message; Father's dead. Hot-foots it home but, transport not being too fast in those days, it takes him a while to get back. By the time he arrives the old man is six feet under and Mum, the grieving widow, has married Father's brother, Hamlet's uncle Claudius. Everyone is out of mourning just a bit too previous, and partying like there's no tomorrow. Hamlet does just what anyone would do, goes into a massive sulk, stomps around dressed in black, very pointedly, face like something that got left in the fridge too long, making snide remarks every time Claudius comes within earshot.

So far so normal. So far, just like Adam, only more restrained. But we know something Hamlet doesn't.

Father's Ghost has been seen on the battlements. When Ghost and Hamlet finally meet, Ghost tells Hamlet that the story put about of his dying of a snakebite is a blind. He was murdered. Claudius did it. 'Avenge me, Son,' says Father's Ghost.

This is just what Hamlet wants to hear. He hates Claudius anyway, always has; now he has a reason, as well as an excuse, for hating him, better still, a reason for killing him. On the other hand . . . on the other hand, killing someone in cold blood is a very big deal and in any case, Shakespeare had another four Acts to come up with. Hamlet spends the rest of the play *not* murdering Claudius, although he kills his girlfriend's father by mistake. If, like Curt, you do not know how it ends, I won't spoil it for you except to add that when Hamlet goes down he takes everyone with him.

The really intriguing thing is, no one else *at all* hears what the Ghost tells him, and he never lets on, even to Horatio, his best friend. As I said, it's just what he wants to hear — but does he actually *hear* it?

He may not even be sure himself. This could be why, when he has the chance to kill his uncle, he doesn't take it. All I know is that when we got to this part at the Theatre Royal, Curt blew his chance to find out. It was dead quiet in the auditorium, on stage.

7

Dark. Claudius kneeling, praying. Hamlet getting ready to knife him in the back but, as usual, starting an argument with himself instead to avoid actually *doing* anything, when Curt wakes up, sees what's going on and yells, 'He's behind you!'

Actors must be trained to ignore that kind of thing, but I'll swear Claudius started to turn his head. At which point Adam shouted, 'Oh, no he's not!' and I – I couldn't help it – joined in. 'Oh, yes he is!'

It wasn't funny. I didn't even think so at the time, while it was happening. It isn't funny now. Wreck a lesson, yes, but not a performance. It wasn't funny, but it *was* the last straw. We were out, right then and there. Next morning we were up; up before Mannion, Head of English; Kumar, Head of Year; McPherson, Head of Everything; who let it be known that we faced suspension, exclusion, were banned from the half-term trip laid on to cheer us all up after mocks, and could expect letters home. That was why I was lurking on the doormat, that Saturday morning.

After we got away from McPherson we were supposed to return to lessons but having nothing left to lose we departed the premises and went round to Curt's since we knew his house would be empty. So would mine, but there were Mrs X's feelings to protect.

Curt's parents do not smoke – anything. How they have gone so long without noticing the herbaceous fragrance that drifts around the lad I cannot imagine, but we went up to the attic and hung out of the window where even nosy neighbours wouldn't notice us. We lit up and discussed damage limitation.

'All we need is time,' Adam said. 'The System is going to get us in the end.' He made it sound like a police state rather than what it was, a bunch of furious teachers and another bunch of unhappy parents, blaming themselves, each other: us, mostly. We'd seen it coming for a long while, Curt had been asking for it, but now it had happened, Adam was right. We wanted time, time to think, time to get ready. Basically, time to lie our way out of it.

What none of us could face was going home and saying, 'You know that trip we were going on . . . which you forked out for . . . Well . . .'

It wasn't going to be any easier when the truth did come out, but if you're for the chop, any stay of execution is worth having. Ask all those guys on Death Row.

The problem was, the trip being planned for half term, parents had arranged half term round it. Mr and Mrs Hague were Eurostarring to Paris for a couple of days on account of I'd be away myself. Mrs Holder, Adam's mother, seizing the rare chance of an empty bedroom, had invited an old friend to stay. The Rules, in whose attic we were toking, were an unknown quantity, and frankly, there was no point in asking Curt. I guessed Mrs Rule would be at home because it was also half term for Curt's little brother who is shaping up badly – runs in the family – and will one day be an even bigger public nuisance than Curt.

'We can't stay here,' Adam said.

'Where are we supposed to be?' Curt said.

I reminded him. 'Cumbria.'

'Where's that?'

The trouble with Curt – and it is trouble – is that it's impossible to tell just how addled he really is and how much he's putting it on. We'd signed up for the trip before Christmas. I assume that he'd known then where we were supposed to be headed, but you could put his own death warrant in front of Curt and he'd sign it. He probably thought he was joining the army. Just how out of it are the Rules, that they haven't noticed their elder son is permanently on Cloud Nine?

'Near the top of the map,' Adam was explaining patiently.

'Canada?'

No, he isn't funny.

'We can't stay here,' I said again, in the hope that someone would make a sensible suggestion.

Adam swiftly dashed the hope.

'We could. Sleep during the day, creep down at night, piss out of the window . . .'

'And live on air like the chameleon—'

'Chameleons eat flies.'

'It's in *Hamlet*,' I said. 'Air and promises.'

'Not for a week,' Curt said, as if he were seriously considering the flies.

I don't live on promises, me. I feed them to other people. 'I promise I'll be home by eleven. I promise I'll do my homework. I promise I'll try harder.' Haven't quite reached the point where I tell the truth: 'All I can promise is, I'll lie.'

'We could go to my sister's,' Adam said.

His eldest sister had got out before the Beast of Bedford came on the scene. She was out already, at University, just altered her plans about coming back afterwards, still living in London.

'Flat in Balham,' Adam said. 'We could crash there.'

'All of us?'

'Just to sleep. We'd be out all day.'

'Doing what?'

'It's *London*,' Adam said. 'There's always something to do in London.'

'Could be out all night too,' Curt droned.

I didn't like the sound of it. Doing anything costs money, especially in London. Anything that does not cost money involves walking a lot: museums, galleries; or sitting. I could see us, wandering endlessly, looking for somewhere to sit down. You can't even sit in the railway stations unless you've bought refreshments. We could spend the week hanging about in public libraries if we weren't careful. Money goes nowhere in London, even if you've got any. I didn't have any beyond what Mum was giving me for expenses to cover the week in Cumbria. My savings account, presumed to contain many hundreds, was down to £13.73. I don't know where it went. It went. Some of it on keeping Curt's suppliers at bay.

On the other hand, where *could* we go between Monday morning and Friday evening? I could probably come back on Thursday, so long as I did it under cover of darkness and hid from Mrs X next door coming in to feed the cats. Adam couldn't go home till Friday, by which time his mother's friend would be gone. Curt had no idea what his parents' plans were for the week, and he'd never have asked. If they'd told him he'd have forgotten five minutes later. I think he had forgotten about going to Cumbria until McPherson told him he wasn't going.

I was trying to come up with alternatives. Pretend to be ill. No – that would involve Mum calling the school on Monday morning to explain, only to get an earful of quite a different explanation. I invite myself to stay with a friend – no. These days there is no one I am friendly enough with to get them involved with lying to *their* parents on my behalf. The only possible candidates were going on the trip and in any case, all these bright ideas featured me alone. We were in this together. It was tempting to blame Curt for his *Hamlet* improv, but Curt had only brought things to a head. McPherson had been lying in wait for something to nail us with conclusively, in addition to bunking off, inattention in class, failing to hand in homework, insolence and suspicion of being under the influence. Only Curt actually abused substances actually on the premises and no one had actually caught him at it.

'We've got to get right out of town,' I said, forgetting that I had not come up with the alternatives out loud.

'That's what I said,' Adam sighed. Being the most

accustomed to surveillance he considers himself an expert at ducking and weaving. 'Did anyone's parents offer to drive them to school on Monday?'

Usually we walk or cycle, but we would have luggage.

'Dunno,' Curt said.

'Dickhead said he would, but I can get out of that. I'll say I'm getting a lift.'

'What on, a skateboard?'

'I'll say I'm getting picked up at the end of the road.'

'Yeah . . . I'll do something like . . .' We were both watching Curt, so far out of the window he looked as if he was going to crawl down the wall, like Dracula.

'How *were* you getting to school?' Adam said, prodding him. 'We're supposed to be there at eight, for the pick-up.'

'It's sorted. Dad's driving me up there.'

'It's *not* sorted. If you turn up for the coach with your old man it'll blow everything.'

'Uh,' Curt said.

'What's your luggage?'

'Back-pack.'

'Then *say* you're getting a lift, with me, and walk round. It's only two streets. They'll believe that.'

'Come round yours?'

'*No!*' Adam was getting angry. 'You *don't* come round mine. You *say* you're coming round mine but you *don't* come. You go to the bus stop and get the 4A into town. We'll meet at the bus station and get the coach.'

'Where?'

'London. We're going to London.'

Things were looking worse by the minute and nothing had happened yet. I kept thinking of *The Great Escape*, that WWII movie. One thoughtless word, from Curt of course, and we'd all be caught out, and massacred.

'Those letters,' I said.

'What letters.'

'Curt, McPherson is sending letters home. Calling parents for interviews. Explaining why we're not going to Cumbria. If they go out today, and they will, they'll arrive tomorrow. They've got to disappear.'

'How?'

'We get to the doormat first,' Adam said. 'We remove the letter. Can you get up in time?'

'I won't go to bed. Easy,' Curt said, reeling himself in over the window sill. 'I tell you, it's sorted.'

For about five seconds he looked alert and confident, and then his eyelids started slipping again.

★　★　★

15

So this was why I stood in our kitchen with those bits of torn paper in my back pocket, smiling innocently at my mother, waiting for the kettle to boil, making idle conversation while I wondered if the Rules' postman had got to their house yet, if Curt *had* stayed up all night, and if he had, would he remember *why* he'd stayed up all night.

And wondering what would happen if he hadn't, if Mrs Rule got to her letter first.

The phone rang.

I'd have rushed to answer it – 'Don't move, Mum. Spare your poor old feet' – but at that moment I was filling the cafetière. Before I could react, Mum was out of the door, back in the hall, mumbling, 'Who can *that* be at this hour?' Good question. It was 7.20 a.m.

On auto-pilot I stopped pouring just before the jug overflowed. Should I barge out crying, 'I expect it's for me'? She'd closed the door behind her, as if she expected the call to be enormously private. Force of habit, I suppose. When Claudius first entered our lives I eavesdropped constantly.

She came back after a minute, looking puzzled.

'It was for you.' I started for the door.

'No, he's rung off.'

'Who?'

'Curtis.' Oh, Christ. What's he said. *Wossesed?* 'He left a message.'

'Yes?'

'Says to tell you it's all right, he got the letter.'

I waited for her to tell me, in addition, that he had informed her what was in it, but she just squinted a bit and said, 'I suppose you know what that's all about?'

'Oh, yes,' I said, with a light laugh.

'Good thing we were up. It's rather early for phone calls.'

Exceptionally early for a call from Curt. 'It's a girl he met, she was over from France on an exchange or something. She promised to write.' Blah blah blah blah . . .

'He rang to tell you *that*?' Looking heavily at the clock.

'Yeah, well, Adam said – me and Adam said – bet him she wouldn't. Write.'

'So it's not all right for you then, is it? How much?'

'Only a burger. It was just for laughs.' I was cursing Curt and his big loose tongue and the spongy remains of his short-term memory. 'I guess he was just being ironic,' I said, and slammed my hand down on the plunger.

I had overfilled the jug after all. A great steaming

brown geyser full of coffee grounds shot out of the spout and went right across the kitchen.

Two

Coming from a different direction, my bus stopped in the High Street, unlike the 4A which goes straight to the bus station.

This gave me five minutes, crossing the town centre, to wonder what was happening to Curt. If he was on the 4A he would be delivered to the door, so to speak. *If* he was on it.

I'd got out of the house without too much trouble since Hague left for work long before I was due to go. Running me up to school would have made him late but he was willing to do it. Somehow I managed to give the impression – or he gave it to himself – that I'd arranged the (mythical) lift to save him the bother.

Mum was hanging around, making sure I'd got everything. I didn't want everything. The holdall was heavy. I'd been planning to empty some stuff out and hide it but Mum knows every item of clothing I possess, down to the last sock, by heart. If I took anything out and stashed it somewhere she might find and recognize it. The fact that everything was bound to come out eventually did not occur to me, or if it did, I discounted it. All that mattered was *now*. Then.

And all I was thinking, cutting down the alley behind Boots, was what we would do if Curt had blown our cover. If he'd blown his own that was his lookout. I was rehearsing more lies, I suppose. But when I came up to the bus station approach the London coach was in and Curt and Adam were lurking nearby, conspicuously trying not to draw attention to themselves.

They aren't the kind of coaches where you have to book in advance, you pay the driver. We shoved our bags in the locker and conferred.

'How much money have you got?' Adam said.

I had £40. Curt, naturally, had no idea and started counting laboriously, finding coins and notes in various pockets. Adam had a hundred.

'I borrowed a Switch card,' he said. I didn't ask whose. Adam's protest movement against the Beast of Bedford involved transparent forms of embezzlement, since if he'd covered his tracks no one would have known he was protesting. Presumably his mother, thinking he was over it, had dropped her guard again.

'Still got it?' Curt asked.

'Mustn't be greedy,' Adam said primly. 'I'll get the tickets.'

'Singles or returns? You save £4 on a return.' Four quid seemed very important at that stage. How right I was.

'Singles are cheaper,' Curt said, cleverly. I'm not sure that he uses public transport all that often.

'Get returns,' I said. 'Even if we end up broke—' I was sure we would '—we'll be able to come home.'

Curt couldn't think so far ahead. He was still arguing about singles when Adam got on the coach and bought three returns. Then we went down the aisle to the back seat where the nuisances always sit. Curt got out his Rizlas.

'You can't smoke on these things,' I said.

'Whaaa—?' He looked round incredulously. Little crossed-out fags on all the windows. 'How long are we on here for?'

'Two hours,' Adam said. 'Don't even think about it, they'll throw us off.'

'Go to sleep,' I said. 'It'll soon pass.'

It was a sensible suggestion. Curt can go to sleep standing up, and does. As he was barely awake anyway he just folded up in the corner and went into one of his comas.

Adam turned to me and said, 'We're going to have to watch him.'

'For a week?'

'I mean it. Otherwise he'll spend everything he's got on stuff. Anyway, he gets stopped on sus every time he passes a cop. That's the last thing we need.'

I didn't want to think about that. 'Did you phone Shanti?' The sister with the flat. The name means Peace, or something transcendental, even if it does sound like a shed.

'Tried to. She wasn't in. Couldn't leave a message on the machine in case she rang back and Mum took it.'

This didn't sound good.

'So she doesn't know we're coming? What if she's on holiday?'

'She isn't. She's going to Greece after Easter, she told us. She'll be at work this week.'

The coach started reversing out of the bus station, and the driver's radio was quacking instructions to him up at the front. It must have been something to do with traffic on the ring road because instead of heading straight out of town he took the northern route.

Adam looked at me. 'You know where this is going, don't you?'

I looked at my watch; 8.10. At 8.20 exactly we passed the front gate of the school. Up the drive, at the main entrance, we could see the hired coach and all our blameless friends in Year 11 standing knee-deep in luggage and Kumar in the middle, yelling something. We couldn't hear her, but I could tell by the way she was standing, her yelling pose. I recognized it at once. I saw it often enough.

And I wished more than anything that I was there with the others, being yelled at. I hated them all, I hated the teachers, I hated the school, but I turned round and watched it disappearing through the rear window and I wished that I didn't hate it, or that I had a reason for hating it, like Hamlet pleased to have a reason for hating Claudius. I knew that Adam hadn't much wanted to go to Cumbria anyway but couldn't resist a week away from home. Curt, frankly, hadn't known where he was going, didn't even know he *was* going, didn't give a toss where he went or who he went with, but I'd been looking forward to it. When Dad was alive we'd all gone up to Keswick once, for a holiday. I'd always wanted to see it again, the lake – Derwentwater, with its little islands, the fells, the pikes, the standing stones at Castlerigg. I probably remember it all wrong; the fells can't be *that* high, the lake that vast, but I'm sure I'm right about the little islands. There's a place on Derwentwater where the trees come right down to the lakeside and you can play around on big stones and roots. I used to look at those little islands and pretend that I lived on one. It had bushes. You could be private there. I saw red squirrels in the trees.

The school party was going to somewhere near Ambleside, but I'd had plans to go back to Derwentwater just once. I wanted to see the little islands again. It would have required a bit of intellectual effort, working out how to do it. I'd half-hoped I wouldn't have to, that the week would include a visit to Castlerigg or Blencathra. I might even have just asked. But there was no one left that I could make myself ask. Asking means going up to someone and starting a conversation. Most of the last term I had been avoiding starting conversations, then avoiding lessons, then avoiding school, almost as if it was coming to get me. Bunking off required *no* intellectual effort. I'd get up every morning, leave the house with a bag of books and kit, then turn right at the end of the road. At the end of the next road the route to school takes another right turn. I'd been carrying straight on, then second left, out of the catchment area. It wasn't so much I was afraid of being seen, I didn't want to meet anyone I knew. I wasn't being defiant and brave about this, I just couldn't bring myself to make that right-hand turn, and once I'd missed that I couldn't bring myself to pass anyone who would know I was going the wrong way. My way took me out towards the ring road. Once through the underpass I knew I wouldn't meet anyone.

What did I do all day? I don't know.

That makes me sound like Curt. 'What did you do all day, Curtis?' 'I don't know.' And he'd mean it.

I just don't know where the time went. If it was fine I cycled around. If it rained I went to the nature reserve which is allotments gone to seed. There are plenty of old huts and one purpose-built rustic shelter. What did I do? What I did mostly was try not to think about what I was doing, what I had done, what I was going to do. But I couldn't help thinking; just being on the move seems to get your brain into gear. What was Hamlet thinking, for instance, on that long trek home to Elsinore? Wasn't he expecting to inherit the crown?

Expecting wouldn't have come into it. The King is dead, long live the King. He must have assumed he was king already. What he was expecting was a king's welcome, courtiers bending the knee and all that. What did he find? Claudius on the throne, under the crown, in the bed. Claudius moved very fast; how did he bring it off? We're never told.

Shakespeare realized this later and shoved in bits about the kings of Denmark being elected, so we'd think he was on the ball all along, and has Claudius telling Hamlet, 'You're my heir. You'll be next' – which doesn't quite square with the election set-up. Maybe Claudius persuaded people that as the kingdom was at war with Norway it was dangerous to leave the executive office empty; they dared not wait for Hamlet.

But Hamlet wouldn't have known that during his long winter ride home. He didn't get what he was expecting. I know how he felt.

Some days I did go to school. I'd get as far as registration, at any rate. Told myself I'd stay and see it out, a whole day. I hardly ever made it past lunch break. We'd go out on the field and that would be that, because if I did get to school, and into the class base, there would be Curt and Adam – on the days when they dragged themselves in too.

Kumar, Mannion and McPherson thought we were in a conspiracy to truant. We never had the energy for that, and how can you conspire with someone like

Curt? It just happened; once, twice. And again. And again.

The coach braked at the traffic lights in Marylebone Road and Curt woke up.

'Where are we?'

'London.' I thought we might have to explain why, but he seemed to remember.

'Sorted,' he said, and started to go to sleep again, but Adam kept shaking him until he was more or less upright.

'Where are we getting off?' I asked.

'Victoria – stay on till the train station, then we can get the Underground. Change at Stockwell.' Adam knows his way around.

The coach stopped in Buckingham Palace Road, just around the corner from the Tube. Curt started to wander off, leaving us to get the bags out of the locker. On his own he would have left his on board without even noticing and there would have been a bomb scare at the coach station.

I bought the Underground tickets and saw that the price had rocketed since I was last there. That happens every time. It was the first mistake, but I wasn't to know that then. I should have got day passes. On the train I had the feeling people were looking at us, but they weren't. This was London. They were *not* looking at us, actively *not* looking at anyone, in case anybody looked back and smiled, or said hello.

On the way out, at Balham, there was a guy selling the *Big Issue* and two more, further along, just begging. There was also a groundsheet and a blanket in the station, dirty but neatly folded, someone's nest. You get the impression that Londoners will swipe anything that isn't screwed down, but I suppose the only people who'd want stuff like that are the other homeless, and I don't expect they'd steal from each other.

I'd thought Balham would be a real dump but it seemed like a nice place to live. Shanti's flat was only a few minutes' walk from the station even going at our speed, which was not great, what with having the luggage, and Curt.

He had one of his flashes of consciousness.

'Didn't you say she'd be at work?'

'Not at this time of day.' Shanti manages a club of some kind. This sounds like fun. It isn't, from what Adam has said. 'Anyway, she gets Sunday nights off.'

No one answered the doorbell at first. Shanti lives on the first floor, so we couldn't bang on the windows or try to get in round the back – if we could have found the back. It's in the middle of a terrace that runs the whole length of the street. Someone was watching us from behind curtains in the bay next to the front door. They didn't exactly twitch but a finger was holding one edge away from the frame. I lost count of time, watching that finger. Adam rang again and we heard footsteps coming down the stairs and the door opened. The finger disappeared.

Adam is tallish, fairish. Shanti is fairish and fattish, but pretty, in a soft, frilly way. She was not looking soft and frilly at that moment, just out of bed, in a huge T-shirt and Teletubby leggings. I mean, there were Teletubbies printed on them. She didn't make you think of nightclub queens.

And she didn't have time to be pleased to see Adam, if she *was* pleased to see Adam, before she saw the rest of us.

'*Now* what have you done?' she said.

I remembered that Adam had landed on her at various times before during his Blue Period, once on the infamous occasion when he eloped with Cara Clements and the police went after them, spurred into action by Old Man Clements venting steam from all orifices.

'Can we come in and I'll explain,' Adam said.

'Who's after you this time?' She was clutching a dressing gown and she started to shrug herself into it.

'No one's after us. No one knows we're here.'

'You said that last time.'

I took the opportunity to butt in. 'Hullo, Shanti.' Curt was occupied in keeping himself upright with the help of some flexible railings that ran up beside the steps and swayed in harmony with him. The finger was back at the window.

'You'd better come on up,' Shanti said. 'Leave that junk in the hall.' Curt showed signs of taking notice but she was referring to our luggage. We lined it up along the skirting board behind somebody's ten-speed, and followed her up the stairs.

When Shanti was a student her place had looked like the sort of state-of-the-art rat-hole that students live in in sitcoms, full of old free newspapers, cans, bottles and dirty coffee mugs, but she'd got her act together. This flat was all pale paint and Ikea. I felt dark and dirty just standing in it.

'Siddown,' Shanti said. 'I'll make coffee.' First of all, though, she closed one of the doors, making me think that it must be a bedroom and that there must be someone in it.

Curt sat down on the sofa and began to read the

Yellow Pages on a shelf by the phone, either to keep himself awake or to look up suppliers. He may have thought they advertize in London. I hung my jacket on the floor and looked at the titles on the spines of a row of books. They were all in French and Spanish. Adam followed his sister into the kitchen and I could hear him starting to explain. I began to hum, quietly. I didn't want to hear what he said.

When he and Shanti came back again, with the coffees, he was still at it.

'Just at night,' he was saying.

'Where? What on?'

'We've got bed rolls.' Fortunately we had. We'd been warned that the centre where we'd be staying offered Spartan accommodation but the food was good. 'We'd clear out before you got home in the morning. You wouldn't know we're here. We won't make a mess.'

'Curt's here, isn't he?' she said. I could see her point. Getting out of the flat in the morning would involve getting Curt out of the flat. Or maybe she was thinking of the mess.

'Anyway, what if Mum rings up and asks me if you're here?'

'Why should she? We're in Cumbria. No one's going to do anything till after half term, next Monday soonest.

We'll be gone by then. We'll be going on Friday – anyway, I've got the mobe. If I ring and tell her I'm at Ambleside she won't know any different. It's only four nights.'

'And four days.'

'We won't be here during the day, honest.'

'Well . . . so long as . . .' She was still looking doubtful but Adam was winning her round. He'd have done it, too, but at that moment two things happened. Two doors opened, the one which Shanti had shut earlier, and the front door.

Out of the bedroom came another girl, nothing Teletubby about this one. She was tiny, little-girl tiny, she looked about ten from the back as she was pulling the door to, behind her. Then she turned round and I saw that she was as old as Shanti, or older. And she'd been out of bed longer, she was dressed for going out and she'd put her slap on. Somehow this grown-up face made her seem even smaller, a tiny woman.

She was just opening her mouth to say something and Shanti was just opening her mouth to say something, when the person at the front door came in. As I looked at him I looked at Adam, and I could see that this wasn't the first time they'd met.

Shanti said, too quickly, 'Oh, Tim—'

Tim – Timothy – is not the sort of name you associate with someone who looks as if he could go fifteen rounds with Rocky even if he is wearing a very sharp suit, but I don't imagine his parents knew how he was going to turn out when they named him.

Tim took us all in with one panning shot and said, 'What's going on?'

'Adam and his friends are having a week in London,' Shanti said. 'They can sleep here, can't they? They'll be out all day.'

Tim said, 'No, they're not staying here.'

He didn't look at any of us, even at Shanti, just walked straight through the room and into the kitchen. The tiny ten-year-old woman blinked nervously and said, 'I'll see you tomorrow,' and scuttled into the hall carrying a briefcase.

Shanti squawked something in her direction and took off into the kitchen after Tim, shutting the door. The front door opened and closed. We looked at each other, then at the kitchen door, listening to the voices behind it, Shanti gabbling again and Tim's voice, flat, loud. 'No. No. They are not staying here.'

She was arguing. He wasn't.

I mouthed, 'Who?'

Adam muttered, 'The live-in.'

'Whose flat is it anyway?'

'Hers and – and –' he flapped his hand at the front door.

'No.' The kitchen door opened. Tim came out. Without looking at us Tim said, 'You are not staying here.' He went into the other bedroom. And closed the door.

Shanti came out of the kitchen and stood in the doorway, chewing her bottom lip.

'I'm sorry.' She said it very quietly, looking at the closed bedroom door.

'What's it got to do with him?' Adam said, but quietly, too.

'Last time . . .' I guessed she meant the Cara Clements affair.

'But that was years ago.' Less than two, actually, I reminded him silently. 'You didn't even live here then. It's not his flat, is it?'

'He helped.' She couldn't take her eyes off that door. 'You'll have to go. I'm sorry.'

'Do you always do what he tells you?'

'I'm sorry.'

We were all looking at the door, now. I was beginning to feel that there was something deeply sinister about Tim and his robotic conversation, and short though I am on chivalrous instincts I didn't like the thought of leaving Shanti alone with him. I was wondering if she was one of those women who walk into doors a lot.

'You'll have to go. I'm sorry.'

Adam went over to Shanti and backed her into the kitchen. They left the door open and I could hear them mumbling to each other, but Curt and I kept our eyes fixed on that other door, as if we were expecting Tim to reappear with a fiery sword to drive us out. Shanti's flat wasn't exactly Paradise, and she hadn't wanted us there, but for a few happy minutes it had looked as if everything would be all right. Now nothing was all right, and with nothing to fall back on I could look ahead, and I knew how safe I had felt, and how unsafe I felt now.

We'd have to go.

We went.

Three

'Who was the heavy?' Curt wanted to know when we were back on the Tube. It took him that long to start wondering. 'The Bad News guy. He knew you.'

'I met him once before,' Adam said. 'He wasn't living with her then.'

'Thought he owned the place. Thought he owned *her*.'

'She's scared of him,' I said. 'Anyone'd think he was her pimp.'

'Shut it,' Adam growled, but that was just how Tim had struck me. Those dead, flat eyes and the dead, flat voice. Did he slap her around? I was glad to get out of the place. I wondered who the tiny woman was but I didn't say anything else to Adam. I don't think Curt had even seen her.

Our most pressing problem was what to do next. We were adrift now, nowhere to go back to and lugging our bags around everywhere. They were getting heavier. Adam was all for stashing them in left luggage, but when we got back to Victoria we found that the lockers there cost £4, even for a small one, which was fine by Adam but Curt and I were hanging on to every penny. It was 20p even to get into the Gents. At least Victoria has seats, a whole block of them near the luggage lockers, which most stations don't, but I didn't think we'd get away with trying to sit on them all night. They were for respectable travellers, passengers, *customers*, not people like us with nowhere else to go.

I kept thinking about that neat little heap in the station at Balham, the folded blanket, the groundsheet. Where were we going to be tonight?

Opposite the station approach is a war memorial and a little park, a triangle of grass with big plane trees. We went across and sat there, with traffic roaring round all three sides, including coaches home, I noticed, and aircraft overhead, making their turn towards Heathrow. On the way in I'd watched them on the flight path, getting lower and lower, ninety seconds apart; officially.

Although it was so early in the year there were already tourists about, and some of the younger ones, our age, were sitting out on the grass. It was warm for February, but not sunbathing weather. Then I noticed that a lot of them weren't sitting, they were lying asleep, and they weren't tourists. They were bundled up as if they were wearing everything they owned and had nowhere to leave it, nowhere else to go. Like us.

I'd seen that park before, often. It gets locked up at night. What happens to those guys then? And I thought about other things I'd seen late at night in London, people in doorways, subways, fast asleep in sleeping bags, under blankets, faces covered. And in broad daylight, some of them. You don't want people seeing you when you're unconscious, although most people walking past take care not to look.

Was that how we were going to end up?

I'd been doing rapid calculations. We'd started out with about £180 between us. Getting to London and then Balham and back had already used up £35 of that; 60p for the gents; £3 for coffee. There was no way we could carry on at that rate, so I didn't think much of it when Adam said again, 'Let's leave the bags and look around. There must be all-night places.'

I said, 'Do you realize how fast the money's going?' I started to run through my listings.

'Yeah, but most of that went on getting here,' Adam said, 'and we don't have to worry about getting back, either, remember? We can't haul this stuff around all day.'

'I'm not leaving mine,' I said. Curt was OK with his back-pack so Adam went over to the station on his own and dropped his stuff. Actually we felt better immediately, just having less to carry between us. We went back down Buckingham Palace Road and round into St James's Park. Curt was like a little kid.

'That's really it? That's Buckingham Palace?'

'You've seen it before,' Adam said, but Curt swore he hadn't. All the way down the Mall he kept looking over his shoulder.

'Look, the flag's up. That means the Queen's in, doesn't it?' I'd never seen him so alert, so we took him over to the lake to look at the pelicans, then up through Horse Guards Parade – 'I've seen this on telly. It's where they do that Colour thing on her birthday.'

I'd never thought of Curt as a Royalist but he was having a really nice time, looking at all the things he'd only ever seen on the box – or only remembered seeing on the box.

We went down Whitehall and stopped to peer through the gates at 10 Downing Street, on past the Cenotaph – 'I've *seen* that, on telly' – and then to the Houses of Parliament, that bit of grass across the road where MPs get interviewed on the news. Someone was being interviewed at that moment. Curt looked as if he was watching history in the making but all we were worried about was keeping him out of camera range. Just what we needed, someone seeing us on the One O'clock News in London, when we were supposed to be somewhere on the road to Ambleside.

When Big Ben struck, Curt just stood and gazed at it. There it was, the world's most famous clock, and he was hearing it, live.

We moved on, over Westminster Bridge, and when we got to the other side we looked back at the view across the river from the South Bank.

' 'tsall muddy,' Curt said.

'Tide's out,' I told him.

'*Tide?* It's a river.'

'It runs into the sea. The Thames is tidal.'

He hadn't known that. It's not tidal at our end of it. I don't think he could quite get his head round the fact that it is the same river.

Then we walked along to the South Bank proper, the London Eye, the Festival Hall, Hayward Gallery, National Theatre. Things began to look up. It doesn't cost anything to get into the National, well, it does if you are going to see a play, but there's huge amounts of space outside the auditoriums, absolutely free.

It was almost like an adventure playground, concrete staircases in all directions, mezzanines – those sort of half-floor-not-quite-balcony things, and terraces. On the ground floor is a bookshop and we even looked around that, a bar, a cafeteria, *and lots of places to sit down*.

We sat around and then hordes of people came out of one of the auditoriums at half-time – the interval – and when they all went back in again Curt, who has no shame, went round swiping unfinished drinks. We took them up to the Olivier foyer and sat out on the terrace and looked down the river to the City, all the new modern buildings behind the old church spires, and St Paul's, poking its dome up like somebody short trying to make sure they get seen in a group photograph.

I remembered that once St Paul's must have been the tallest building in London. You'd have been able to see it from miles away like you can see Canada Tower, down at Canary Wharf. I thought if we were stuck for something to do tomorrow we could go and have a look round down there and get those day passes for the Underground that let you go on all London Transport – like we ought to have done today. We could spend all day on the Underground, if we had to.

There was still tonight to get through. It had started to rain.

The school coach would have arrived by now, we reckoned, so while it was still quiet we took turns to ring home on Adam's mobe. Adam went first. His mother took the call and, listening to his fluent untruths about the journey and the weather and the accommodation, I began to pray that the Rules would be out when it was Curt's turn. I went after Adam and got the answering machine. Oddly enough, it was harder to lie to that than it would have been to lie to Mum or Hague. You have to know if you're getting away with a lie while you're telling it. I ummed and erred and burbled, but most people do that anyway when they expect a human and get a machine instead. It probably sounded convincing.

I handed the mobe to Curt and waited while he remembered his own number.

'Hi, Mum. Yeah, got here hours ago, no . . . well, I dunno. Half an hour. Yeah, sorted, yeah. Great. Yeah . . . yeah . . . *yeah*. See you. Sorted. Bye.'

'Sorted,' he said again to Adam, as he handed the mobe back. I suppose they're used to him at home. Maybe they think everyone talks like that.

People left after the afternoon performances and later on another lot started to arrive for the evening ones. I thought of the actors, flaked out between shows, how fast the time must pass for them, how slowly it was passing for us. The evening crowd were a lot more dressed up. There was a jazz group playing downstairs in the main foyer, round the grand piano, so we went down and listened to that. When the auditoriums opened we did what Curt had done before, cruised around and collected drinks; there were sandwiches and pizzas this time, too.

Then we noticed two guys behind the bar eyeing us up and down and looking pointedly towards another bloke who had Security written all over him, so we decided to move on to the Festival Hall. More food, more booze, more jazz.

But even that closed down eventually and we were out. It was still raining and now it was cold.

'I suppose Scrooge here doesn't object to spending money on the Tube to get back to Victoria?' Adam said, to Curt, but addressing me.

'Live dangerously,' I said. We were all slightly sloshed from the cocktail of leftovers we'd been necking since mid-afternoon, and got lost trying to find Waterloo Underground. I had a feeling it was in the main station but we couldn't find that, either. Everything is being rebuilt round there. We kept going up steps and along walkways, through tunnels, and everywhere we went there were voices at knee level, 'Got any spare change?' I wondered, were they going to sit in the rain and darkness until everyone had gone home? London may be an all-night city but it was looking very empty that particular February night.

In the end we came out on Hungerford Bridge, the footway across the river next to the railway lines between Charing Cross and Waterloo. The City still looked magical away to the east, lit up and reflected in the river, but there were no lights on the bridge. It was like crossing two pages of a graphic novel, Batman or something like, all dark girders and menacing silhouettes and shadowy figures, highlights on the rails. About halfway across is a puddle. I remembered Dad telling me that that puddle has been there since *he* was a kid. We all walked through it, me first. Even though I knew it would be there I didn't see it coming, and we were still stumbling over legs in sleeping bags. 'Have you got any spare change?' And every time I knew, all over again, that we'd never last a week like that. Too sudden. Too soft – us. It's something you descend to, I suppose. No one goes from home comforts to sleeping on the streets overnight.

We had to wait ages for a train although there are two lines through Embankment Station; another £3.60 down the drain. We could have walked to Victoria but we didn't feel like it by then and when we got there we discovered something we hadn't thought about. Victoria was closing down for the night. All the shops and bars were shut, and the left-luggage place was almost deserted except for cops, moving on people who had nowhere to go.

'Let's get out before they get to us,' I said, for I'd noticed, from the way the cops were talking to the crusties, that they probably knew a lot of them and both sides went through this routine every night.

But they didn't know us, three lads looking dead suspicious, loitering with intent. Shifty. As I said before, Curt tends to attract the attention of the Law every time he passes one and I didn't know what he had on him, although I could guess. We were all of us swaying on our feet, fatigue and booze, and if Curt hadn't had a spliff all day he was almost certainly in possession of the ingredients. We slithered out again and stood under the overhang at the top of the steps down to the Underground.

'When does that close?' Adam said.

'Dunno, round midnight, I think. Half past.'

It was around midnight. In the distance Big Ben began to strike and at the same time there was a surge of sound overhead. We looked up and through the cloud layer we could see lights moving in a slow arc, as the aircraft they were attached to made its turn on to the flight path for the airport.

'I know where we can go,' Curt said. He moved out from under the station canopy to stand in the rain and watch the lights as the clouds closed in below them.

'Florida,' Adam jeered, but I knew what Curt was thinking.

'That's landing, not taking off,' I said. 'Heathrow.'

'That's right,' Curt said. 'Let's go to Heathrow. Airports never close.'

'How?'

'Piccadilly Line,' I said. 'The trains are still running.'

'Just. Don't let's hang about.'

We changed at Earls Court and got on what was probably the last train running that evening. It took a long time to get to Heathrow. Underground trains never move as fast as you think they do, although this one ran overground and was non-stop, part of the way. It was quite crowded to start with, people were using it to get home on, but by the time we left Hatton Cross we were the only people in the carriage.

We'd been watching that strip of map above the windows, counting off the stations. There are two at Heathrow. Terminal 4 is the first, but I thought we ought to stay on till Terminals 123 which would give us room for manoeuvre if we had to keep moving. The only time I'd ever flown from Terminal 4 was when I went to Canada with Mum and Dad. We'd taken the coach to the Central Bus Station and then caught the little airport shuttle. I didn't know if it ran at night, but I did remember that Terminal 4 is a great bare hangar of a place.

The station was empty. No one else got off the train.

'You sure it doesn't shut?' Adam said.

I was wondering the same thing. When we got up the escalator to the concourse it was all deserted, nothing but those long lines of interlocked trolleys like Chinese New Year dragons, and the gaping mouths of the tunnels to the terminals. I looked up the stairs to the Central Bus Station. It was so quiet I could hear the rain, but I could also hear a bus, up there on the wet tarmac. Then I heard an aircraft taking off and a clash behind me. The other two were getting a trolley out, only Curt had started at the wrong end of the dragon. At least trolleys are free at Heathrow. We'd spent another £10.50 getting here from Victoria.

'Which way shall we go?' Adam said, too loudly. There didn't seem to be anyone around to overhear, but I thought we'd attract less attention if we at least seemed to know what we were doing.

'Terminal 3,' I said. 'There's more going on there. It's for the international flights.'

'Where do the rest go?' Curt asked. He really wanted to know.

'Terminal 2's for Europe. 1's for the UK.'

'But we're in the UK.'

'And Ireland. But you can fly to Scotland and—'

'Can you?'

You could fly anywhere, Curt, I thought. You don't need an aeroplane.

We loaded the trolley and set off down the tunnel. I was feeling very worldly by now. *I* knew my way about. Even Adam didn't really know much about this place, he'd only ever flown from Gatwick and Stansted. Curt, though, was worrying me. It wasn't so much what he didn't know as what he had forgotten. I remembered how much he'd enjoyed himself looking round London, as if he'd never seen any of it before. I could believe he'd never been to Heathrow, but he seemed so clueless about airlines in general. Still, it had been his idea to come here. Would I have thought of it if he hadn't got in first?

I'd always taken an interest in flying, probably because Dad used to fly so often. When he took us abroad Mum seemed to enjoy flying, well, not to *mind* it, but when he was away on business she spent her time glued to the radio, listening for news of disasters.

He died in an aircraft, but it hadn't crashed. It was still on the runway at Düsseldorf, waiting in a queue to take off, when the guy sitting next to him noticed something was wrong and called the steward who had to broadcast for a doctor. There were two on board, but no one could do anything. Dad had had a cerebral haemorrhage, there in his seat, just closing down his laptop before take-off. The flight had to be aborted and the aircraft taken out of the queue, but Dad was dead before they even got him off the plane. The guy who was sitting next to him was Mr Hague; Claudius.

Among the other things Curt didn't know about was travelators. He couldn't believe it. Fortunately the one going the other way was out of order or he'd have been doing the kind of thing kids do on escalators, running up the one going down.

There used to be the names of all the places you could fly to, along the walls of the tunnel, but it's all being rebuilt and the walls were bare. At the end of the travelator it was just concrete, with wires dangling from the roof. Adam wanted to go back to the Underground concourse and find a more promising tunnel to explore but I urged my party on to Terminal 3 and when we arrived I knew I'd made the right decision. The Check In concourse was almost as deserted as the station, but it wasn't actually closed. There were people about and no one gave us a second glance. We had luggage.

Thank God we had luggage. One of the first things you learn at school when you want to kill time is, *never go anywhere empty-handed*, even if it's only wandering over to the pencil sharpener with a pencil that you've sharpened six times already. Later, when you start to bunk off lessons, if a teacher sees you walking down a corridor during class time they will jump on you immediately. 'What are you doing/where are you going/who gave you permission?' If you are carrying something you look legit. A piece of paper or a book won't do, it's got to be something substantial, a pile of papers, an armful of books, folders, boxes; not under your arm, that looks too casual, but in both hands, in front of you if possible, steadying the pile with your chin. I did it with a guinea-pig cage, once.

That's how it was with the luggage. We had a trolley, we had luggage, therefore we looked as if we had legitimate business in an airport, entitled to be warm and dry, entitled to sit down.

There were a few places to sit, so we sat. Curt started to doze. Adam looked ready to flake out too, after all, it was ten to two in the morning. People are supposed to be closest to death between two and four, I've heard somewhere. I could believe it, looking at Curt.

I left them to guard the luggage, though with the state they were in anyone could have walked off with the trolley, and went up the stairs, halfway along, to the Departures area.

Ten to two in the morning and the joint was jumping. Well, not quite jumping, but heaving up and down a little. I could see why when I looked at the monitor. A flight to Hong Kong had been massively delayed, so massively that rather than get trapped in the Departures Lounge from which there is No Return, a lot of passengers had stayed out here, eating and drinking.

No one was going to notice us.

I sat down at a table where there was a whole pile of cups and cartons. No, I didn't finish any leftovers, I was past that. All I wanted to do was look as if I was a paying customer. I toyed with half an oozing burger, but that was just for the look of the thing. I couldn't believe what I had swallowed during the day – the previous day; it was tomorrow already.

That made me feel better. The first night was taken care of. It wasn't over, but the end was in sight. That left three days and three nights. If we divided our time between Arrivals and Departures, and went to a different Terminal each day, we could go on not being noticed. And now we didn't have to worry about paying for somewhere to sleep, we could eat properly; we didn't even have to stay in the airport, we could go places; day trips.

I remembered the luggage. Perhaps one of us could stay with it while the other two went out. Would I trust Curt alone with my hold-all? I didn't know if they'd have Left Luggage at an airport. Mostly you say goodbye to it when you check in except for what you carry on to the aircraft.

There are strict regulations about the size of hand baggage but if the worst came to the worst we could pretend that what we were lugging around was hand baggage, given the size of some of the stuff that people shove into the overhead lockers. I don't quite know what worst I was expecting.

The lavatories are very well-appointed, and *free*. When I came back I found Curt and Adam just where I'd left them, and dead to the world. You look so defenceless when you're asleep. You *are* defenceless, of course. I thought of those people in the doorways in London, sleeping the days away with their faces covered, and I wondered what would happen to them if they tried doing what we were doing, how soon they'd be sussed.

I was so glad we had that luggage.

I sat down and assumed that I'd go to sleep too, but I didn't. My mind was whirring, like I was high on something. I could almost feel vibrations. Maybe it was because I was doing all the thinking for the three of us. The more I tried to sleep the more awake I felt, no, not awake, just past sleeping. Quite bad, really. Someone had left yesterday's paper on the next seat so I leafed through it. Adam and Curt went on sleeping, Curt snoring a bit. In the end I got my wash bag and towel out of the hold-all and went to the Gents again and had a good wash and a shave. I look much older unshaven but unshaven looks dodgy. You need to be able to get up a good head of stubble if you want people to think you've *chosen* not to shave.

I felt better after that. I went along to the designated smoking area and had a cig. I didn't just feel better, I felt normal, the sort of bloke you wouldn't look twice at, so I strolled outside and stood in the dark, breathing aircraft fumes. No one asked me what I was doing. I heard a plane coming in and checked my watch. It was 5.30. The first night was over.

Four

When I got back to Check In Curt was awake and looking around him, blinking, as if he wasn't quite sure where he was. Possibly he wasn't.

'Heathrow,' I said. 'Terminal 3. Departures. Remember?'

'You look different,' he said.

'I washed. Get your things out of your bag and do the same – no, hang about.'

I shook Adam, by the foot. He told me once that this is how his mum wakes him up. I didn't want Curt wandering about on his own.

Adam woke up with a jump and then flopped back again while reality hit, or seeped in.

'Where've you been?' he said. He noticed I was carrying the paper. 'You might have bought us coffee.'

'No, do this properly. Go and have a wash and brush up in the bog and then have some breakfast upstairs.

We can afford it, now. I'll stay here and mind the bags.'

'All my stuff's at Victoria,' he reminded me.

'Take mine – but don't use my toothbrush.'

'Have you had breakfast?' Curt said, as if I'd somehow beaten him to it.

'Look, unless we're going to cart these bags around with us everywhere we'll have to take turns at everything. I went upstairs while you two were asleep. Now I'll mind the stuff while you go.'

They shuffled off, Curt swinging his Boots gentleman's toilet bag like he was going to brain somebody. I didn't think he needed to be so obvious about it but no one took any notice of him. To be honest, I was quite glad to see them go. I'd liked being on my own. I thought I'd have a kip while they were gone, but I still wasn't tired. Actually, yes, very tired, but not sleepy. I did the crossword in the paper, but they say you only need a reading age of seven to get through that one. I ought to have bought the *Guardian* but Claudius takes that. He usually does the crossword in about twenty minutes. I've never even finished it once. If I ever directed a modern-dress version of *Hamlet* I'd put that in, only the other way round, Claudius getting stuck on 9 across and Hamlet, not saying anything because there is nothing in the text referring to crosswords, naturally, just picking it up and finishing it and then tossing it back to his uncle in a scathing manner.

Quite a lot of *Hamlet* sounds like crossword clues, when you think about it:

3 down. Very like a whale, 5 letters. Cloud – or camel. Not a hawk, 7 letters. Handsaw.

What builds stronger than a mason, a shipwright or a carpenter? 11 letters. Gravedigger.

The company paid for Dad's body to be flown home and Claudius accompanied it. He was the one who phoned from Germany to break the news. At least he had the sense not to ring Mum direct, but called Head Office, and they sent someone down who knew Dad.

Mum went to pieces. I was at school and when I came home there was this strange woman in the kitchen and a doctor, not our doctor, someone else I didn't know, coming downstairs, and Mrs X (the cat feeder) from next door. She had come round to help but, out of force of habit, I suppose, she *had* fed the cats. Mork and Mindy were ear-deep in Arthur's Choice Cuts. The strange woman was making tea.

I'd come in quietly. None of them had heard me arrive until I showed up in the kitchen doorway. 'What's going on?' I said. Then I began to take in the strangers.

'What's happened? Where's Mum?'

I never even thought about Dad, well, I wouldn't, would I? He wasn't meant to be there. He was in Düsseldorf. I thought Mum must have had an accident, there was blood on the kitchen floor.

They were all looking at each other, the doctor trying to come in and get out at the same time, the woman from Head Office not knowing what to say, and Mrs X knowing just what to say but not how to say it.

She said, 'Sit down, Russell,' but there isn't really anywhere to sit in our kitchen except bar stools. She steered me round the doctor and into the living room. I was getting angry, and frightened.

'Has Mum had an accident?' I wouldn't sit down.

'No, not your mother. Your father's been – he's – he died this morning. We've just heard.'

Well put, Mrs X. I was impressed, later. *He's dead* sounds so stark, shocking. *He died this morning . . .* well, oddly enough, it put the ball back in his court, like dying had been his decision, he'd done it himself, he hadn't had it done to him.

All I could say though was down to years of Mum's conditioning. 'Not in a plane crash?'

That was when I discovered he'd actually been on

an aircraft when it happened. Mrs X is very all right. She didn't do what a lot of people would have done because they'd read the right books or seen a documentary, insisting that I sat down, drank hot sweet tea, took this pill, waited till later. She sat down herself, so of course, I did too, and then she answered all my questions, none of which I can remember except the last one.

'Where's Mum?'

Mum had let the woman from Head Office in and when she heard the news, started *screaming*, so loud that Mrs X, who was out the back getting the washing in, thought she was being attacked and burst through the hedge carrying the first weapon she could lay hands on which was, when she came to look, the pickaxe that Mr X had been using to break up some old concrete standing.

She'd got badly scratched about, coming through the firethorn. That was where the blood on the kitchen floor had come from. Thinking about it later I guessed that that was why I'd thought of Mum having an accident, and how I'd known the strange bloke on the stairs was a doctor. Mrs X was really deeply cut – firethorn spines are like stilettos – but she said she didn't feel a thing at the time.

She didn't even notice until she got home again what with being frightened half out of her wits by the screams, and wondering what she'd find when she got to the house.

Mum, she told me, was upstairs resting, under sedation. They always say that after murders on the news, and I'd always assumed it was a lie to keep ghouls at bay, but it was true, this time.

'What do you want to do, Russell?' she said. 'Tell me what you want. I'll see to it.' The woman from Head Office came in with the tea. Mrs X waved to her to put it down and she went out again.

'I'd better phone Gran,' I said. Mum's mum, that is. Dad's mum died when I was quite small. Gran is young for someone my age, and tough. She would take over and come down to look after us – and break the news to Dad's dad. Big Daddy, we always called him, for a joke, because he is as thin as a mike stand, and he is no joke. He'd had a bust-up with Dad when he married Mum and he's never seemed very interested in us. I couldn't face ringing him.

'Do you want me to?' Mrs X said. Phone Gran, she meant.

'No, I'll do it.'

I did. Meanwhile Mrs X got rid of the Head Office

woman, nicely, of course, she'd been pretty shaken, too, nipped back next door to finish getting in the washing and leave a note for Mr X, and came back with a bottle of Scotch. We both had a big one, sinful for me, underage, and sinful for her, five months pregnant. She really had been *valiant*, grabbing the pickaxe and smashing through the hedge like that in her condition. She made me swear never to tell Mr X what she had done because he would go ballistic if he ever knew the risk she had taken, putting his wife and son in peril (she'd had one of those scan thingies so she knew it was a boy even then). I swore, and I kept *that* promise at least, though I always thought it was a pity that Mr X never knew how brave his wife is. He'd be an idiot if he didn't know that anyway.

Later on Gran and Grandad arrived and the next morning Big Daddy turned up, and all the time Mum just lay upstairs crying, or out of it, under sedation. I went to school, not out of hard-heartedness; it was something to do. No one seemed to need me around.

And then, at last, Dad came home, and Claudius came with him.

After an hour the Departures area was filling up; people, trolleys, queues at the check-ins. Adam and Curt came back looking fully human again, not surprisingly – *they'd* had a proper breakfast on top of several hours' sleep.

They were still carrying towels and stuff which would draw funny looks anywhere else, but not here, apparently. Adam started repacking and said, 'We've got to find somewhere to keep this lot.'

'We keep it with us,' I said.

'You're joking,' Curt said. 'Remember what it was like yesterday?'

I was quite surprised to hear him talk about remembering and even more surprised to catch him doing it, memory not being his strong point. But he hadn't had a spliff for about thirty-six hours. I don't know how long the effects take to wear off, not in the quantity he consumes it, but I believe you never recover lost brain cells. Perhaps his were resting up a bit.

'No, look,' I said. 'This is an airport. People are here to travel. They have luggage.' This was an understatement. Looking at what the queueing trolleys carried, some of them seemed to be shifting furniture. 'We've got luggage. So long as we've got it we're going to look as if we've got a right to be here.'

'A lot of them upstairs didn't have luggage,' Adam said.

'No, they'd checked it in. What *they've* got are tickets, boarding passes. Which we haven't.'

'If you think we're going to spend the rest of the week toting this stuff about everywhere—'

'We don't have to go everywhere together. So long as one of us stays with the bags, the others can go off where they like.'

Curt had wandered away, as he does if you aren't actively eyeballing him. I muttered to Adam, 'You or me, that is, with the bags. If he goes off on his own we may never see him again. I mean, look . . .'

Curt was breathing on the window and making footprints in the steam with the sides of his hands and fingertips. Ever tried it?

Adam went and fetched him back. I went across to one of the American Airlines desks that didn't have a queue and got baggage tags, which made our stuff look even more official.

'Now what?' Adam said.

'We've been here long enough. Now we go to Arrivals.'

'What's at Arrivals?' Curt said. Forget about those rested brain cells.

'It's another *place*, that's all. We can stay there for a bit. I'll stay, you and Adam can go walkabout. You can go to London, if you like. Pick up Adam's bag from Victoria.'

'Aren't we in London?' Curt.

'No, we aren't in London, we're nearly in Slough,' I told him. 'When you come back we'll move on to Terminal 2, get it? That's where we'll be tonight.'

'You got all this worked out?' Adam said. He didn't seem too pleased, mainly, I thought, because going to London had been his idea and it had been an embarrassing failure. And now I was taking control. I wasn't trying to.

'While you were asleep,' I said. 'We don't *have* to do it. I just thought it would be easier, safer, never stay too long in one place; different terminal each day, half in Departures, half in Arrivals.'

'What about yesterday?' Curt said. I pretended not to hear.

'Where do you want to go, Curt?'

'Where is there?'

Even from Curt this wasn't as moronic as it sounds. You can't *walk* out of Heathrow, it's surrounded by roads. Even if we were nearly in Slough, we *weren't* in it, or Uxbridge. Anywhere we went would require public transport.

'Get the Underground. Why *don't* you go to London, have a day out—'

'You're the one who's suggesting—'

'Just be careful. It's got to last.' If Adam hadn't had so much more than me and Curt I'd have suggested pooling resources. 'We haven't got to pay for board, have we? But we've still got to eat and travel.'

First off, though, we had to shift to Arrivals. It's a separate building and much smaller, since nobody would want to hang about there much, even if they end up having to. It was still early, but stiff with people who'd come to meet other people, some of them carrying cardboard signs with company names on. There were others with signs written in marker ink on what looked like torn-up cereal boxes, and there were scads of foreigners who were expecting to be met and hadn't been. We settled our bags in the corner of the coffee shop. On the way in I'd noticed a left-luggage place, but I kept quiet. Luggage made me feel secure.

'Where do we meet you?' Curt said, very pleased to have thought of this by himself.

'Here,' I said. 'I'm not shifting your gear over to 2 by myself.'

'When?'

'Five o'clock? And bring back some food, it costs a

fortune here. And don't go anywhere you can't get back from.'

'Anything else?' Adam said, nastily. 'What are you going to do all day, then?' He sounded as if he thought I was planning something underhand, more underhand than what we were doing already, that is.

'I'll think of something. I brought a book.'

'What for?' Curt said, honestly curious.

'To read on the coach to Cumbria.'

'But we aren't—'

'Take him away, Adam.'

I got rid of them at last. I really did want to see them go. I'd been looking forward to being alone again, as I had been earlier, over at Departures. But what I'd had then I didn't have now, that sense of freedom. What I had now was the luggage.

I bought a coffee and tried to find something else to read in the paper. I was saving the book for later; I wanted to make it last and I'd already started it.

Time passes so slowly when you're trying to make it pass. Every time I looked at my watch it was two minutes since I last looked at it. I walked all round Arrivals twice, looked in all the shops and found another coffee place and bought another coffee – and that was another £1.50 gone. When I saw 10p lying on the floor I pounced on it.

At ten o'clock I couldn't stand it any longer. I fetched a trolley, loaded the gear on to it and went outside. I avoided the tunnel to the Underground concourse in case the lifts weren't working, instead I walked across to the bus station and sat there. It was cold but at least it wasn't raining. I wanted a cigarette badly, the more so because I had a packet. Nine left. We'd been told not to take fags to Cumbria and as for *drugs* . . . I wondered how Curt was managing without any kind of smoke entering his lungs. I swore not to light up until evening because if I ran out I couldn't afford to buy any more. It was terrifying the way the money was leaking away. Even if we weren't paying for somewhere to sleep everything cost much more here at Heathrow – that is, it didn't seem possible to buy anything that was cheap. Perhaps flying makes people feel rich.

Even if it doesn't, there's nowhere else they can go.

All the time I was sitting in the bus station there was a tremendous roar every couple of minutes or so as a plane took off, and the air was heavy with that stink of aviation fuel that makes paraffin seem as pure as vodka by comparison. The Terminals are so far from the runways that you don't get much of a view, but there in the bus station I could see the planes as they climbed, not the take-off part which is what I really like to watch, but the moment when they go into the steep bit, gravity-defying, that enormous machine, nose-up, straining to get into thinner air as soon as it can.

I know all about *how* they get off the ground; they go up because they *have* to go up, it's the climb that looks impossible. I was always having to explain take-off to Mum, that the aircraft isn't driven into the sky, like a rocket. It's the air beneath its wings, lifting it, but she was never convinced. She *wouldn't* understand. I thought I was putting it badly at first, my fault, but in the end I realized she didn't want to; understanding something so technical didn't fit in with the way she thinks of herself, as though if people knew she could get her head round manly things like aerodynamics, they would start to expect too much of her.

It works, you know. When Dad died Mrs X and Gran and Grandad and even Big Daddy (where he couldn't avoid it) stepped in to take over, made the arrangements, and Mum just wafted around being helpless and prostrated and collapsing. And then Claudius arrived and she collapsed all over *him*.

Which is very much how I imagine Gertrude, Hamlet's mother, carried on when someone came and told her that her husband had been bitten by a snake while he was having a kip in the orchard.

Gertrude would have come over all faint. 'Is he badly hurt?' 'Very. He's dead. Very dead.' And swollen up too, probably. So she passes out. Everyone rallies round, takes charge, sees to things; Polonius, Osric, Cornelius, Voltimand, and her ladies in waiting.

Then, *Enter Claudius*. Where was *he*, up to this point, I wonder? The Ghost says that Claudius was the one who poured poison in his ear, or Hamlet thinks he does, but what was Claudius doing at Elsinore anyway? The King's brother, just hanging around making himself useful? He certainly made himself useful afterwards. 'Here, little lady, lean on me.'

And she leaned.

Gertrude is so wet. You might say, well, women were like that in those days, or men wanted them to be like that; but they weren't. Look at Queen Elizabeth I; look at Shakespeare's women come to that, Lady Macbeth, for starters. Macbeth wouldn't have got very far if he'd been married to Gertrude. Macbeth would have come home a bit glassy-eyed and said, 'I met three old hags who told me I was going to be Thane of Glamis and it came true. Now they say I'm going to be King.'

'Oh, darling, that Glamis thing was just coincidence,' says Gertrude. 'You can't be King. Don't be silly.'

'It's Fate,' says Macbeth, furrowed brow.

'You know it's no good talking about Fate to me,' says Gertrude, Fate being to her what aviation technology is to Mum, something male and complicated.

So Macbeth has a beer, reads the paper and gets an early night. End of story; end of play.

And if Claudius had had Lady Macbeth to contend with he wouldn't have lasted five minutes – Claudius in the play, that is – unless, that is, she'd put him up to it in the first place.

Our Claudius didn't work as fast as Hamlet's uncle. At first I hardly noticed him, the house was so full of grandparents. I spent lots of time next door with the Xs whose name is actually Xanthopoulou. When I was younger I couldn't understand why Mum and Dad called them Mr and Mrs X because I thought it ought to be Mr and Mrs Z, naturally enough. They are Jane and Theo in real life.

Most of what I remember clearest about that horrible day was Mrs X coming to the rescue with the pickaxe, ready, for all she knew, to find herself confronting an armed robber or a rapist.

'I didn't stop to think,' she said afterwards. 'You don't, when something like that happens.' I know plenty of people who would stop and think, and then decide that it was none of their business, they didn't want to get involved; or dial 999 and then sit twittering until someone else arrived and sorted things out.

She could easily have said to herself, 'I owe it to my unborn child to stay out of this.' The unborn child is thirteen months old now, Nicky, a bit of a blob as yet. I hope he grows up worthy of his mother. When he is older I shall take him on my knee and say, 'Listen, Nicholas, you are the son of a heroine.' And he'll wriggle about and pick his nose and won't hear a word, I expect.

I counted my money again, glad even of the 10p I'd found under the table in Arrivals. It was lunchtime. Lunch was out of the question, but I reckoned I could rise to another coffee. I strolled back to Terminal 3 very slowly, back to the café, found a different place to sit, and treated myself to a bit of my book. I read that very slowly, too.

I was getting really tired by now, I kept blacking out, not in a dead faint but the way you do on a long journey, falling asleep for a few seconds and then waking up with a jolt. I got the impression that people were giving me funny looks – no, it wasn't an impression, they *were* giving me funny looks. *Why?*

Then I realized that I was staring at them and *they* were feeling spooked. One lady actually moved her chair out of my line of fire. She had a baby with her and was expecting another. She looked much too pregnant to be flying. I hoped she'd be all right. Maybe she was meeting someone.

I might have gone right to sleep and no one would have noticed, but I couldn't. There'd be a sudden noise, or someone would knock against my chair, or trip over the trolley and pile it up against my shins. I was starting to feel light-headed, I couldn't concentrate on what I was reading. After an hour I'd still only got through four pages and I hadn't a clue what it was about. I decided that when we shifted ourselves to Terminal 2 I'd buy a book of crossword puzzles, and then I remembered that I couldn't afford it. Maybe I could nick one. Maybe not. The last thing I needed was to be arrested for shoplifting. That made me think of security cameras. Was one watching me? If someone monitoring it decided I was acting in a suspicious manner, things could get awkward.

A bit of a gap had opened up in the crowds, maybe there'd been a lull between 747s and only a little plane had landed. I looked up and saw Adam coming towards me. Five o'clock already? Time must have been passing faster than I'd thought. I expected Curt to lurch into view as usual and got up to meet them, but there was no sign of him. Surely Adam hadn't lost him? Adam knew as well as I did that Curt on the loose was a dangerous scenario. For a start, would he ever find his way back? Would he forget where we were and just go off and get the coach home?

Then I noticed it was only ten past three and they'd been due back at five.

I said, 'Where's Curt?'

Adam sat down. 'Only got himself arrested, didn't he?'

'Arrested? What for?' The first thing that crossed my mind was Possession. He'd been stopped often enough. I often marvelled at the police man-hours wasted on stopping idiots like Curt on the off-chance that he looks like someone who is carrying something he shouldn't be. But it wasn't that.

'Shoplifting,' Adam said. 'In Oxford Street.'

'What were you doing in Oxford Street?'

'Just looking around. We were in one of those big stores with lots of little cafés in them, but you couldn't smoke in any of them. It was opposite KFC.'

Some of those Oxford Street stores are a whole block

long, and all he could remember was that it was opposite KFC.

'Selfridges?'

'I dunno, it was big. Anyway, we were just coming out and some sort of bleeper went off at the door. I didn't think anything of it, I just kept going, I mean, there were three or four people coming out with us. Then I realized he wasn't with me. I looked round and there were two blokes with him in the doorway, then they all went back in. He didn't even try to make a run for it. Didn't even *try* to.'

'What did he take?'

'I don't know. I didn't see him take anything. I mean, what is there to take?'

'In Selfridges? Quite a lot.'

'Yes, but nothing he needed. We hadn't been in the food hall. We came out through ladies' hosiery, all those legs.'

I had a sudden wild and horrible thought about some secret life that Curt had been leading that involved ladies' hosiery, but I had to admit that, knowing Curt, he wouldn't nick anything useful anyway. I could just see him grabbing handfuls of stockings, because they were there, or rushing off with one of the legs.

'*Why, Curtis?*'

'*Because it was there.*'

'Then what happened?'

'When?'

'When they took him back inside? What did you do?'

'Do? What could I do?'

'You mean, you just left him there?'

'I didn't have much choice, did I?' Adam said. 'If I'd gone back and said I was with him they'd have thought we were in it together.'

'I thought we *were* in this together.'

'Oh *yes*, you'd have gone and said, "Excuse me, I'm with him. We're supposed to be in Cumbria with our school but we got banned from going so we're hiding out at Heathrow and we thought we'd drop in on Oxford Street for a spot of nicking." '

I thought about that. If the store had got the cops in, and they probably had, Curt would have been arrested and first off they'd want his name and address. What had he told them?

What I took care not to wonder was what would happen if he had confessed all. That involved thinking ahead. I was not in thinking-ahead mode. Heathrow was my layby, out of the fast lane.

'What did you do then?' I asked, wondering for the first time what Adam *had* done. 'Just bugger off and leave him?'

'I waited,' Adam said. 'I waited for ages. I went across the street, just in case. I went into the KFC and sat in the window, but he never came back. Those places, Selfridges and that, they're huge, they've got dozens of doors. The cops probably went in round the back – and came out that way. I didn't know what to do. In the end I went back to Victoria and got my bag and then I came back here.'

'I suppose we'd better hang on, then,' I said. 'They're bound to let him out after they've charged him.' Poor Curt. Those West End stores are full of professional gangs, but it had to be him who got caught.

Adam bought more coffees and we hung around for another two hours. Then we went outside with the trolley and had a cig. It was getting dull, the way it does in winter before it gets fully dark. Still Curt didn't show up.

We still had his luggage.

Five

We went underground with the trolley to Terminal 2 and surfaced at Check In. Unlike the one at Terminal 3 it's dead straight and very long. It is also very plain and functional. Right at the far end, past the Air France desks, were a few seats. Adam had brought some cheapo food back with him so we sat and ate it although it was still quite early and I wasn't hungry.

I ought to have been, but I was beginning to feel really strange. No sleep last night and not a lot the night before on account of having woken up half a dozen times full of alarm about what might happen next morning when we made our getaway. I was starting to have those mini black-outs again, but every time I was on the verge of dropping off Adam started talking. He was really on edge, feeling guilty about leaving Curt and worrying, like I was, about what Curt might have said.

I couldn't blame Adam for not going back. Adam has form. Soon after the Beast moved in and before anyone noticed how Adam was taking it, Adam had also taken a car. It was the Beast's car. He loaded the little sisters in and set off round the ring road driving in a manner that caused eleven separate concerned citizens, including three lorry drivers, to grab their mobes and alert the police. Adam was intercepted at the A40 turn-off.

The Beast behaved like a gentleman on that occasion and declined to prosecute, but Adam had committed an offence so it couldn't end there, quite apart from the fact that he could easily have killed himself, the little girls and anyone who happened to get in the way.

The idea, Adam said later, was that the Beast would take the hint and go away. This did not happen. The family exists in a state of armed truce at the moment. The girls are settling down. The trouble was, from Adam's point of view, they hadn't minded the Beast at all to start with, and they don't mind him now. Adam had turned them and now they have turned back. The littlest one calls the Beast Daddy. Adam is the Lone Rebel.

The Lone Rebel was dozing again. The crowds were thinning out so I left him with the trolley tucked up close to him and went for a stroll all the way to the end of the Check In hall. On the way back I saw an escalator to Departures so I cruised up for a look. That was all I needed, one look. This was where we had to be. Terminal 2 Departures was big and warm and full of comfy chairs. There were shops, a post office, even a games arcade. I sat down, just to enjoy it on my own for a few minutes, but I kept wondering what we were going to do if Curt had spilled the beans. Would the Rules, Ma, Pa and Little Monster, all descend on whatever cop shop he was in and haul him home, or would they come here and look for the rest of us? Or would they tip off Adam's mum and the Beast? Mr and Mrs Hague would be in Paris by now, with any luck. I wished I'd paid more attention to their plans when Mum was explaining them to me, but I was too busy implying that their concerns were no concerns of mine.

The Beast was only called the Beast because he came from Bedford. He could have been the Halifax Horror or the Thing from Tring. Dunno what he might have ended up as if he'd come from Canterbury. But it was Bedford, so he was the Beast. I'd never seen any evidence of him being beastly; he didn't knock Adam's mum about or molest the girls or even raise his voice to them much.

'What's wrong with him?' I asked Adam once, all innocent, before the Hague wedding.

'He's *here*, isn't he?' Adam snarled. 'He's here and Dad isn't.'

That was the big difference between me and Adam. His parents split up long before the Beast hove into view. Adam kept hoping that his father would come back but he was one of those statistics that lose touch with their kids within two years. I never even had that hope.

I might have done if Dad had been around more. Like people who lose a leg but go on feeling their toes, you hear about people who *know* their parents or husbands or lovers are dead, but keep expecting them to walk in at the door. I knew Dad wouldn't be doing that. He'd always come back from his business trips before but often late, because of airline delays, especially in summer, with all those extra holiday flights cluttering up the skies, so it didn't seem strange his not being there, because I was so used to him not being there. That's not to say I didn't miss him, I always missed him, but there again, I was used to it. And what I was even more used to was being the man of the house, not in a hairy-chested way and not in an I'll-give-the-orders-around-here way either, because I was a schoolboy and not earning anything. I'm not a complete prat. And where would I have learned to act like that? Dad never did.

But Mum was always consulting me. 'Shall we do this? What do you think about that? Would this be a good idea?' They were never things she couldn't have worked out on her own but when there were just the two of us there and Dad was away, she made me feel I was part of the running of the house, that what I thought and wanted *mattered*. Though to be honest, when it came to serious decisions, like whether or not to call a plumber, it was usually Mrs X who had the casting vote.

And when we knew Dad wasn't coming back I assumed we'd go on like that only for real. I wasn't looking forward to it, I just took it for granted that that's how it would be, which is why I'm certain that all the way from Wittenberg to Elsinore, Hamlet assumed he was going home to be King.

Neither of us had reckoned with Claudius.

Mum didn't need my advice and, looking back, it wasn't *me* she was thinking of when she asked for it. She just wasn't up to the responsibility of making a decision on her own in case it was wrong. She must have been brought up like that. She still calls Gran and

Grandad 'Mummy and Daddy' and even when Dad was alive she was always on the phone to Gran, asking her about stuff like what curtains to buy. Gertrude's parents must have been dead or she'd have been on the sixteenth century equivalent of a phone all day.

Carrier pigeons, perhaps.

One of the few sensible questions Curt ever asked about *Hamlet* was, 'Suppose he hadn't seen the Ghost?' although he wasn't trying to be sensible, he was being awkward.

Yes, what if? The Ghost doesn't have a lot to say, but if he hadn't told Hamlet about the murder what would have happened? Never mind the problem of getting through the next four Acts, what would Hamlet have done? He'd have just gone on skulking around the place, making life hell for everybody and then, I suppose, he'd have got the horse out of the garage and gone back to Wittenberg with Horatio, to finish his degree. And eventually he would have become King when Claudius died, married Ophelia . . .

Not much of a story. But I can't just think of them as characters in a play.

I've never given much time to thinking about *Macbeth*, even though we read it in Year 10, because you never really get the chance to see him being good before he goes to the bad, but *Hamlet*, everything's happening before your very eyes; there's so much going on. So much, that Shakespeare loses track of it himself, half the time, like how old Hamlet is or how long Horatio's been back in Denmark, but these things don't matter. What we're seeing is someone actually cracking up, bit by bit. What we don't see is what started it all – not the murder, the moment when Hamlet arrives home. You can imagine, he's been rehearsing all the way, going over and over in his head what he'll do when he arrives, young King Hamlet, what he'll say to his mother, what he'll do at the funeral – no. He must have known he'd never have been in time for that.

Lucky Hamlet. Dad's funeral was horrible . . . but at least it wasn't ludicrous, like Ophelia's.

There are a lot of deaths in *Hamlet* but only one funeral, Ophelia's, Hamlet's girl. It starts with a gravedigger and a passer-by talking about suicide, and whether Ophelia drowned herself or not. It's a sort of comedy routine, believe it or not.

But it's all very sad and serious after that – until the fight. Ophelia's body is brought in with Gertrude and Claudius who are both genuinely upset (he isn't *all* bad) and Ophelia's brother Laertes, who is upset and furious. When he sees Hamlet he really goes apeshit and they have a punch-up *in* the grave, on top of the corpse. Laertes has good reason. He blames Hamlet for the death of his father – hard to deny, we see him do it, on stage – and the death of his sister, driven mad by grief at losing her father and being thrown over by Hamlet. Well, he's right there too. When Hamlet does finally decide to avenge his father's murder he doesn't care who gets in the way.

No, Curt, he doesn't win. He doesn't deserve to. From where Laertes is standing, he's no better than Claudius.

Our Claudius was at Dad's funeral. It was the first time I'd seen him properly. The one time he came to the house before that he was just one stranger among lots of others coming and going. At the crematorium there were loads more people that I didn't know, from the office, and Dad's friends and family; cousins I'd never heard of let alone met. Claudius stood out the way a good actor does in a crowd of extras, even if he's the shortest one on stage. Before he's done anything you notice him, what they call Presence. Claudius had presence, *has* presence, although I don't much notice it any more (all I wanted then was his absence).

We were in the front row, me, Mum and Big Daddy, nearest and dearest, and I ought to have been paying attention to the coffin and the vicar, but I'd noticed Claudius and I kept turning round to see if I recognized him because I was sure I'd seen him before. I had, but it was only afterwards when we went back to the house, that I found out who he was and why he was there.

Even so, I wasn't sure why he *should* be there, it was only family and close friends, otherwise. I didn't have the nerve to go up and say, 'Who the hell are you?' and in the end Mum, who was doing the brave widow bit very well (she'd had a veil at the crematorium, for Christ's sake) beckoned me over and said, 'Russell, I want you to meet Christopher Hague. Christopher, this is my son, Russell. David's son. Russell, Christopher was with David when – when –' She started weeping again and everybody turned to look and then turned again and didn't look and Claudius stooped – he's very tall – and put his arm round her. I'd been about to do that myself and there was no reason why I shouldn't have gone ahead and done it, but seeing him get there first – I *couldn't*. Both of us with our arms round her – it would have been like admitting that we had equal rights.

When I told Adam about it later he said, 'After the insurance money.'

★ ★ ★

Adam was waking up when I went to fetch him and take him upstairs. It was ten o'clock and things were fairly quiet. I began to wonder what it would be like at Terminal 1 tomorrow. Perhaps internal flights don't leave at night and we'd look suspicious. They might even close Terminal 1.

'You could *live* here,' Adam said, when I showed him the Promised Land at the top of the escalator. He headed for the comfy seats. 'Have you had any sleep?'

'No, you have.'

'Your turn, then. I'm going for a slash. Want a coffee?'

'No, tea.' Coffee's meant to keep you awake. Perhaps it was all the coffee I'd drunk and all the food I hadn't eaten that was stopping me sleeping. Perhaps a really huge meal would do it, or a lot of booze, but I couldn't afford either. In the end I would just fold up. I'd have given anything to do it right there, but it wasn't going to happen. I was starting to discover exactly what light-headed means. My head felt very large, and very empty, and very brightly-lit, like a hot-air balloon. I didn't feel as if I had a skull, whatever was separating the inside from the outside was extremely thin and fragile and seemed to hurt all over. Most headaches are internal; this one was on the surface, stretched out all over it like clingfilm, as if the head itself was some kind of horrible swelling, a gigantic zit, and if I pressed hard enough with both hands, it would burst.

Or stuck a pin in it. In the Middle Ages doctors did a kind of brain surgery called trepanning, cutting a hole in the skull to let out the evil humours, and I've heard that some people these days trepan themselves with a Black and Decker. I'd always thought they must be nuts, but just then I could imagine drilling a hole in my enormous head and what a relief it would be.

You often see pictures of Hamlet holding a skull, as if that's the only memorable thing he does, like he carted it round with him and brought it out sometimes to, like, break the ice at parties, but in the play he only handles it for a moment, in the funeral scene, after the gravedigger unearths it and then tells him who it belonged to, someone he'd known when he was a child.

He doesn't drop it in horror. In those days death wasn't something you pretended would never happen, *could* pretend would never happen, because no one you knew had ever died. You lived with it, took it for granted, counted yourself lucky to live long enough to die of old age.

Dad was only forty-six, and very healthy, we thought. He must have thought so too. It did cross my mind that he might have known he could die at any moment, but it seemed he didn't. He hadn't taken out any massive life insurance or anything like that. He *was* insured, of course, but not for an amount that would have tempted anyone to murder him. After Adam suggested that Christopher Hague was hanging around hoping to collect, we got into this stupid, stupid game about how he was the murderer and it was all a foul plot to get at the money by marrying Mum.

There was no question of his marrying Mum then, but something happened a week or two later.

The ashes were in a sort of vase thing – no, we didn't keep them on the mantelpiece alongside Auntie Nellie's appendix in a jar of formalin. Mum had them in her bedroom, somewhere. I suspect she was putting the vase on the dressing table and *talking* to it. I could hear her voice, sometimes, when there were just the two of us in the house and I was in the living room, doing my homework.

I'd always done it downstairs when Dad was away, to keep Mum company, but she wasn't wanting my company at that time. I didn't blame her, in fact I was feeling very grown-up about being able not to blame her. And partly I was thinking, What about me? How do you think I feel? But she wasn't thinking about me. Very Gertrude.

What did Gertrude *think* would happen when Hamlet got home and discovered that she'd married his uncle? She didn't think. She never does. She wants everyone to be happy and nice to one another *and she gets over things very quickly*.

I kept suggesting ways we might cheer ourselves up, not being callous, just not sitting around being miserable. I thought we might go and see some brain candy at the multiplex, or go out for a meal, or a walk in the country even, things we usually did together when Dad was away, but she only said, 'Not yet, darling. Soon. Not yet.'

Then I came home from school one day in December and she was out. First I thought Yippee! because she had actually gone and done something all by herself. Then I thought that the thing she had gone and done might be to drown herself. I really did, and I started running around, looking for notes. We used to write each other messages with a marker pen on the white tiles over the kitchen sink where we'd be sure to see them, but I didn't somehow think that anyone would write *Goodbye cruel world* on the wall with a felt tip pen. Certainly not Mum.

I was about to go round to Mrs X, to see if she was there, and knowing that even if she wasn't I'd get some

TLC, when a car pulled in at the front gate. Not our car. I froze, I was so frightened, but then the door opened and out got Mr Hague. He shut the door, walked round and opened the passenger door, like a chauffeur. Mum got out.

Dad never did that. It would never have occurred to him to open car doors for able-bodied women, and Mum would never have expected him to. It struck me later that she'd been waiting for Hague to do it, that she knew he would. He'd done it before.

He closed the door and zapped it with his gizmo, but then Mum looked at the front door, not at me looking out through the window, but at the door. She'd seen my bike. She said something to Hague who had started walking towards the house; put a hand on his arm. They both stopped, said a few words. Then they parted, she came towards the house, he got back in the car.

I knew what had happened. Seeing my bike reminded her that I was home from school, she having forgotten, after two years, that we come out early on Wednesdays, and she didn't want me to know she'd been out with Hague – or didn't want a confrontation. She didn't know I'd seen them.

I went down fast and opened the door before she

could get her key in the lock, and in time to see the car reversing out into the road.

I said, 'Who was that?'

She said, 'Mr Hague. He was at the funeral. The man who brought David home. The one who was with him when he died.'

Usually, at this point, she'd start to cry, but not this time. She just smiled sadly.

I said, 'Where've you been?' I thought it must be something to do with work – Dad's work; some sort of tidying up.

She said, 'We went to Blewburton Hill.'

And I knew why.

Six

Adam came slouching back with my tea and a sandwich. I didn't offer to pay and he didn't ask me to; we both knew he had a lot more cash. He'd got himself a juice and sat blowing bubbles in it through a straw.

I said, 'I wonder what Curt's doing?'

'What are we going to do with his luggage?' Adam said, and kicked the back-pack.

We were thinking the same thing and it had nothing to do with luggage. What had Curt been saying?

'Want a ciggie?' Adam said. We moved to the designated smoking area but five minutes after we sat down Adam was asleep. I didn't know how he did it. The walk had woken me up all over again and the hot-air balloon feeling was back, like my head was full of swollen blood vessels, about to rupture. A cerebral haemorrhage, in fact. I wished I hadn't thought of that.

Hot-air balloons was one of the things we used to

see from Blewburton Hill, those and aircraft taking off from Heathrow, especially Concorde. When I was little I used to go there with Dad, just the two of us and I thought it was because *he* was mad about aeroplanes seeing that he spent so much time in them, but he just loved going there. He used to act excited if we saw a balloon or Concorde, for my benefit; he got a kick out of my kick, really. What he loved was watching the sunset over the Berkshire Downs. We always went there in the evening. As I got older we did it less often but we still made it up there two or three times a year.

The odd thing about Blewburton Hill is that although you get an amazing view from the top, it isn't all that high, and unless you know it's there you hardly notice it. There's a triangulation point on top, in a concrete block, 110 metres, but the downs are much higher. It's an old hill fort, with terraces carved out round two sides. There are walnut trees growing there, that was another thing we went for, in autumn. In a good year you could pick up loads, still in their green husks, and Gran would pickle them.

Dad put up with me leaping about, 'Oh, look, there's a rabbit, there's a MacDonnell Douglas DC10, here comes Concorde!' What he liked to do was stand on the hill looking out over the Thames Valley, all the way across to the microwave tower on Beacon Hill. If we stayed late we could see the red lights on it come into view, and it glowed like a massive star rising. In the other direction is Didcot Power Station, and slowly that lit up too, and gradually lights would come on all over the valley.

Dad said jokingly, more than once, to Mum, 'You can scatter my ashes up there.'

That was what she'd done, that was where she'd been.

Why hadn't she taken me with her?

I could have understood her going off alone, it would have been thoughtless, selfish, but I *would* have understood it. But she'd gone with *him*. What did she think she was doing? She didn't think.

Gertrude.

When she told me she'd been to Blewburton Hill I was supposed to ask why. It would have been reasonable because all the times Dad and I had gone up there she'd come along only once or twice. It wasn't her kind of thing, climbing hills and watching aeroplanes; or her kind of place. That was why I guessed the reason and that was why I didn't ask. Let her do the talking.

'I'll make some coffee,' I said, 'feed the cats.' Mork and Mindy were not due to be fed till 4.30 but if the house has been empty they go into a starvation routine, trying to force their way into the cupboard where the tins are kept. The lower part of the door, where it meets the frame, is scratched to shreds. It's only for show. I don't know what they'd do if they ever got in unless Mork, who is a bruiser with six toes on each foot, has found out how to operate a ring-pull.

Mum followed me into the kitchen. I'd missed my cue, not only failing to ask why she'd gone to our hill, but why Hague had gone with her, this bloke we hardly knew – allegedly.

'It was such a lovely day,' she said.

'I remembered how often David said he'd like his ashes scattered there,' she said.

'Chri – Mr Hague – said at the funeral, if there was ever anything I wanted doing, *anything*, any time . . . so . . .' It was getting sticky. I rattled the Go–Cat box.

'And it seemed a good moment . . . it *was* a good moment, the right time . . . to let go, there on the hill with the sunlight and the breeze . . .'

Hullo, blue sky, hullo, green grass. Hullo, worms.

While all this was going on I was filling in my lines in my head. *Why didn't you drive yourself there? Why didn't you take me? We should have done this together.* She *can* drive but she doesn't unless it's unavoidable. The car had been in the garage since Dad left for the last time.

I can't drive. Born too late. Bad mistake, that.

'I hope you stood upwind,' I said.

That was unforgivable.

I couldn't forgive myself, that is. After all, it was Dad we were talking about. But I remembered a ghoulish story about some people who went up on a cliff to scatter ashes and, not thinking, flung them into the ocean breeze and ended up with the dear departed in their hair and down their necks.

'Oh, Russell, you don't *mind* do you?'

'Oh, Hamlet, you don't *mind* do you? I mean, there was all this food left over . . .'

There's this line in the play when Hamlet tells Horatio what he found when he came home. *The funeral baked meats did coldly furnish forth the marriage tables.*

'. . . all the guests – I mean, mourners, were here already, so we thought we might as well kill two birds with one stone.' Beautifully put, Gertrude.

But I knew Mum was feeling guilty which poor old Gertrude never does. When she saw my bike outside the front door and started wondering how I'd respond to a visit from Claudius, she sent him away. I didn't say anything else about the ash-scattering on Blewburton Hill; not then, not ever, even after I went to look.

At about six I stopped trying to sleep and stopped trying to read and went off to the Gents to do the ablutions. Then I went and bought a coffee. This time yesterday I'd just felt relieved because we'd got through the night. Now we'd got through two nights but I wasn't feeling doubly relieved. Physically I was feeling wrecked and in addition I had the Curt problem to worry about.

I got another coffee for Adam and did a quick tour of Arrivals at the far end of the concourse. Things were busying up, lots of noise and announcements over the PA. Even so, as I came towards Adam I heard his phone start to ring, the first bars of Beethoven's *Ode to Joy* played on elastic bands. I accelerated, trying to yell 'Don't answer it!' quietly, but before I could reach him he had it out – I think he located it by instinct in his sleep – and was saying, 'Hullo?'

Then, 'Hullo, Mum.'

'Ambleside.'

'Yes – no – I—' Then he shut up and there was clearly a lot of talk going on at the other end. I could guess what that first exchange had been.

'Hullo?'

'Adam!'

'Hullo, Mum.'

'Adam, where are you?'

'Ambleside.'

'No you're not.'

'Yes—'

'You're lying.'

'No—'

'Where *are* you?'

'I—'

'I know what's been going on etc etc etc.'

When the etceteras finally ended Adam said, 'No, he's not,' in answer, I suppose, to 'Is Russell with you?' Then he said, 'London.' Then, 'Victoria Station.' Then, 'No, he's not. Honestly. I don't know where he is.'

There was more talk from his mother. I spent a lot of time repacking my stuff until they'd finished. Adam switched off before he put the phone away.

'Curt talked?'

'Not much,' Adam said, 'but when his parents found out they got in touch with mum. What about yours?'

'Out of the country.'

'*They* phoned Cumbria last night and found out we

weren't there either. Sorry, Russ, your cover's blown too.'

'Yeah, but you didn't say where I was. Thanks, pal.'

'How d'you know?' He really thought I hadn't been listening.

'You said – Oh, I guessed. What's happening?'

'I said I was at Victoria. They're coming to pick me up.'

'When?'

'Right away.'

'Are you going to be there?' For a second, no more, I thought I might go with him. Then I knew how relieved I'd be when he'd gone and I'd have no one to think about except me. I could go home when I felt like it, or not go home at all.

'Might as well. Can't give her any more grief,' Adam said.

He meant his mum. He thinks a lot of her – she thinks a lot of him, in spite of everything. And what had she done to deserve the grief he'd already dished out? Waited six years after her useless lying pig of a husband walked out and left her with five kids, waited six years before finding someone new. *She waited.*

'Better not hang about, then. It takes about an hour to get back. I'll walk you to the station. Drink your coffee as we go.'

Down we went to Check In, got a trolley and returned to the travelator, the tunnel, the Underground concourse.

'I'll take Curt's backpack,' Adam said.

'No need,' I said, nobly.

'I'll have to. I mean, he'll need his stuff anyway, but his parents know I was with him. They'll expect me to have it, won't they? Funny he never let on we came here, isn't it?'

'He probably never knew,' I said.

Adam went and got his ticket. I saw him frisking through his wallet and then he came over and passed me two notes, a ten and a twenty.

'How do you know I'm not coming with you?'

'You're not, are you?'

'No.'

'Get some sleep. You look like you've been dead for a week.'

He hooked himself into Curt's back-pack, started to pick up his bag, then gave me a quick hug, muttered, 'See you,' and barged through the automatic barrier, kicking the hold-all in front of him. I watched him disappear down the escalator but he didn't look round again.

I was so surprised by that hug. I wished Adam was my Horatio, the closest friend, the absolutely-trusted one, but as I watched him go all I could think was, *Rosencrantz and Guildenstern are dead.*

Rosencrantz and Guildenstern sound like a firm of solicitors or a comedy act, which they are in a way, although what happens to them isn't comic. They are Hamlet's friends, the sort of friends you have when you're a kid because their parents know your parents. Rosencrantz and Guildenstern were at school with Hamlet, but Hamlet never has much to say to them, not like he does to Horatio. When Claudius tries to stitch Hamlet up by sending him abroad, he uses Rosencrantz and Guildenstern to carry secret letters that will lead to Hamlet's murder, but Hamlet, being naturally suspicious, discovers the plot and substitutes letters of his own. Right at the end of the play we find out what happened to Rosencrantz and Guildenstern.

Not that I would have done anything like that to Adam and Curt, or they to me. We *are* friends, but I can't see us staying friends for ever and ever. We're friends because we sort of drifted together and got into trouble together and our parents have always thought the other two were evil influences. Bit by bit people at school left us to each other because, to be honest, we are not a whole lot of fun to know. None of us has even got a girlfriend at the moment. And who is the influence; Curt with his doped-up refusal even to think, or Adam, lashing out in all directions and not caring who he hurts, or me? I don't think I am a particular influence, but I'm the third leg of the stool. I shore the other two up. They probably wouldn't hang together if I wasn't there as well.

So it was ridiculous to think of Rosencrantz and Guildenstern when Adam went off down the escalator, except that I didn't care. That's why I was so surprised by that hug. I didn't think he cared, either. Hamlet doesn't like Rosencrantz and Guildenstern and they don't like him. It's quite obvious to everyone, except Gertrude, of course, that they don't give a toss about each other.

And mostly that's how Adam and Curt and I feel, but if we didn't have each other, who would we have? Before I started bunking off school with Curt and Adam I did it on my own. I never asked anyone else to come with me and no one ever said, 'Where were you, yesterday?' (Well, teachers did, but not people.) I didn't want anybody with me, especially not the first time, when I went to Blewburton Hill.

I cycled and I had my school bag with me, that first time, because I hadn't left home intending to bunk off. There's a grassy strip and a bit of lay-by on the Aston Upthorpe road where people park. I padlocked my bike to the fence, hid the bag in the bushes and walked up the footpath between a paddock and the great sweeping field that runs down towards Blewbury. The last time I'd come was in late August, with Dad, and the combine was out. Now it was sown with winter wheat, just a film of green shoots. The chalk there is so close to the surface the soil is almost white.

It seemed odd being there in the morning. The rabbits had gone underground for the day and the only signs of life were a couple of horses in the paddock and they weren't the kind to come over to watch you in the hope of being given sugar. There's a double fence to stop that kind of fraternization, I think it's a stud farm. When I got to the stile at the end of the footpath I did what we had always done, walked along the lowest terrace of the earthwork, then scrambled up diagonally to the next level, then to the top, you can't call it a summit. It's almost flat but gently curved, like the top of a gas holder.

Then I just stood and looked all around at the downs, and the valley, across to the Chilterns and back to Didcot Power Station, and nothing looked quite right because I was used to seeing it all lit from low down in the west, by the evening sun. There were planes taking off from Heathrow but it was the wrong time of day for Concorde. I'd always loved seeing it heading into the sunset, neck stretched out like a swan, and dwindling into a golden flash that hung in the sky.

Dad never got to fly in Concorde although he said he dreamed of doing it. I used to think I might do it for him, once.

I walked around among the cowpats and thistles, wondering where he was, where Mum had launched him from. Had he become airborne, dispersed, settling like dust miles away, or had she poured him out carefully, like salt? Was he down there, underfoot? Was I walking on the remains of my father?

Where *was* he?

When we were little we got the bit about heaven at school, the afterlife, I'd call it now. When people I knew about died I suppose I believed it when someone said, 'Granny's in heaven, now,' but when you're little you don't know many people who die, not in this country, at any rate. After a while I realized that whether or not

I believed it, when I thought about them I didn't imagine them anywhere, not in heaven, harps and clouds, not being reincarnated; definitely not in hell, flames and pitchforks. I didn't think, don't think, that they are somewhere around, in spirit; they aren't. They are not. They *are* not.

To be means to live. *To be or not to be* means to live or not to live – Hamlet's famous question when he walks in talking to himself. The edition I read, there are three pages of notes about what this speech means. It would be easier to understand if we knew what he's been thinking before he starts talking. Has something happened to set him off? He says being dead is no worse than being asleep *but* what if you dream when you're dead? Suppose death is one long nightmare?

Long before I came across *Hamlet* I knew that whatever I tried to believe, I thought about death as *not being*. Nothing. Not anywhere. I didn't feel that Dad was somewhere around, hovering over Blewburton Hill because his ashes were there. Dad was gone. There was no more David Jagger.

But there *was* Christopher Hague. It wasn't that time when I started thinking about Gertrude and Claudius, him up on the hill with Mum when it ought to have been me, but it was soon after, when we began to see more of him, that is, she did.

I wonder what I'd have seen and felt up there if I had believed, had had some kind of faith in the afterlife. Would I have seen the ghost of my dad, rising up against the hills, calling, *I am thy father's spirit; doomed for a certain term to walk the night* . . .

Another time I came home and found the house empty I went round to see Mrs X. Do I sound pathetic, a big boy like me getting in a snit because Mummy isn't waiting at home to give him his tea when he comes in from school? It wasn't like that. Mum used to have a job, running an office, and depending on what the workload was like on any particular day, she was often out when I got back. No problem. I'd make coffee, start on homework, feed cats. All that stopped the day Mrs X came through the hedge with the pickaxe. Mum had got the afternoon off because Dad was due home that evening. She never went back.

Even then I thought it was a mistake. I had school. It didn't stop me thinking about Dad, I didn't want it to, but it stopped me thinking about him all the time. Going to work could have done that for Mum and I think they held the job open for her, but she never did go back.

So when I came home to an empty house and saw

our car still in the garage I went next door and asked Mrs X if she knew where Mum was? I didn't expect her to know, I just wanted to sit and talk to her. She was eight months gone by then and sitting around more. I don't want to give the impression that she spent her time snooping out of the window, spying on us, because she didn't, but her living room looks out at the front, like ours does. She might have seen . . .

She had, except that she wouldn't have noticed especially, she said, if Mum hadn't waved over the hedge as she got into the car—

What car?

The car. His car.

'David's friend,' Mrs X said. 'He was at the funeral.'

'He wasn't his friend,' I said. 'He just happened to be in the next seat on the plane.' Then, 'Does he often come round?'

'I don't know,' said Mrs X. She wasn't fudging, she didn't know. She hadn't noticed, she wouldn't lie.

We had a cup of tea which I made to save her getting up again.

'I'm not that frail,' she said, and laughed. We both knew she wasn't frail – I thought of the pickaxe – but she let me make the tea. She's nice like that. While we were drinking it Mum came back, on foot, so I wouldn't know where she'd been, who she'd been with. I did wonder where he'd dropped her off. She was carrying something, but I couldn't see what it was over the hedge.

It wasn't that I minded her being out – I didn't want her sitting at home all day, being melancholy like I said, but I minded her trying to fool me. I said goodbye to Mrs X and went home.

Mum was upstairs and came down as I shut the door.

'Where've you been?' we both said at the same time.

I said I'd just been next door and she said, 'I thought I'd go into town for a bit. You won't bother Jane too much, will you?'

You don't bother your real friends by going to see them.

Later on, I saw a carrier bag in the swing bin; Russell and Bromley. She'd been buying shoes. I wondered who'd paid for them.

Seven

When Adam disappeared down the escalator I went up to the bus station to find the shuttle to Terminal 4. I'd originally meant to leave Terminal 4 for the final night but it didn't make a lot of difference where I went, and I was going to be a lot less conspicuous without Curt and Adam.

The bus station was bigger than I remembered and I couldn't find the shuttle, but I discovered that there were some ordinary service buses that went to London but stopped at Terminal 4 on the way, and you could travel for free. Heathrow seemed more and more like the Never-Never Land. Whatever you wanted was there.

There weren't many people on the bus and I could sit and look out of the window. It takes about ten minutes to get round to Terminal 4 and you start to realize how enormous the airport is, and most of it is space; not space for people, space for aircraft. It's the elbow room above the ground that matters. Seen from the air the whole thing is like a mutant Star of David, miles wide. I saw an old map once, it's at home somewhere, showing that part of West London as rough open land, Hounslow Heath. Crossing it is a crooked little lane with a few houses scattered along it. A row of houses on the heath. Heathrow.

I looked out of the bus window across the runways, and wondered where those houses had stood. You lose all sense of direction there. It wasn't until I saw an aerial map of the layout that I realized that all the airport buildings except Terminal 4 are in the middle of the star and that the entrance road goes under the runway.

Then we were right outside the complex and I could see the tail fins of BA 747s, the long-haul jobs. I started looking at the other people on the bus, then, real passengers, real travellers, with somewhere to go. But if any of them were looking my way I must have seemed the same to them.

The bus stopped outside the Check In area and as soon as I went in I saw that I'd come to the wrong place. When I'd been there before, with Mum and Dad, it had been bedlam. Now it was almost empty.

There was nowhere to hang about and, unlike the bus station, it wasn't nearly as big as I'd thought it was, and there were hardly any shops or seats. The idea, I suppose, is to get people into the Departures lounge as soon as possible, and out of the way, to avoid the kind of chaos you get at the other terminals. Chaos was what I needed, though, especially when I spotted the Law.

There was an escalator going up to Arrivals and I was walking towards it when I saw these three cops standing at the foot. They were chatting to each other in an off-duty way, not even watching people, but just seeing them was enough to make me nervous. In fact my nerve endings seemed to short-circuit, giving me a real jolt in the guts. I was about to change direction but I was thinking fast enough to realize that this *would* look suspicious, and managed to keep moving, past the cops and up the escalator.

Half-way up there was a landing with one of those imitation pubs crammed on to it. Like everything else in the place it was almost empty and there was a dark unoccupied corner. I was just about to go in when I thought, Maybe they're watching me, and I quarter-turned round.

The cops were not watching me, but one of them was on his way up the escalator, a few steps behind me.

Brain went into overdrive. If he was on my tail and I went into the pub I'd be trapped. If I kept moving on up I'd at least stand a chance of losing him, even if it meant dropping the bag and making a run for it. I kept moving up, praying that there would be crowds of people in Arrivals.

Fat chance. Arrivals was the same as Departures, long, empty, no where to hide. Opposite me were the exit doors. Could I reach them in time? In time for what? I looked round. The cop wasn't behind me any more, he was still on the landing, talking to someone. Ve-e-e-ery casually I walked on to the far end of the concourse where there was a coffee shop and a few seats, few enough to make you understand that you needn't stay too long. I bought a coffee, the cheapest kind which was not at all cheap, and sat down next to a woman with a baby in a sling against her chest. I didn't want coffee, couldn't afford it, but the sight of the Law had rattled me. I really did feel rattled, literally; shaken up inside and everything loose. My legs didn't feel joined on any more. I was thinking of Curt, I guess. Guilt by association.

I calmed myself down by watching the baby, fast asleep, not a care in the world. Safety by association.

There was a big window next to the seats with the

view of the tail-end of a BA 747, one of those with pictures on the stabilizer. I stared at the pattern, at least it was something to look at. It seemed to be all squiggles and dots, kind of insulting to put on the tail of one of those beautiful aircraft. If I didn't blink, the dots and squiggles started to shift about like some horrible virus mutating under a microscope. When I looked away my eyes were full of dots and squiggles and through them I saw that the three cops were now standing at the top of the escalator. Or maybe it was three different cops. I looked away, for a quick reassuring fix of sleeping baby, but the baby had gone and out of the corner of my eye I saw that one of the cops was heading in my direction. I didn't wait to see if it was actually me he was heading for. I picked up the bag and started for the exit.

We passed each other with a couple of metres' clearance and I was convinced he was watching me, but when I got through the door I was still on my own and still seeing spots. I'd stood up too quickly and I had to stop and wait for things to settle down. I felt really sick for a few minutes.

I thought I'd come out where I'd gone in but, of course, I was on a different level. As it turned out, after a few seconds' panic, this was just as well as the buses only set down at Departures. From Arrivals they pick up. I found the shuttle stop and waited there for the bus, shivering and gulping until the sick feeling went. Then I just felt horribly cold and tired. The sky was darker than I'd expected, like night was falling. We must be in for a storm. When the shuttle came I crawled on board and curled up in a corner. I never wanted to move again, but six minutes later we were back at the bus station and I had to get out. I meant to go back to Terminal 2 and the comfy chairs, but on the Underground concourse I took the wrong tunnel and ended up at 3. I had just enough energy to get upstairs and along to the coffee shop near the Departures gate.

It's an odd layout up there. A great sweeping ramp runs down to the security check. The first time I saw it I was much smaller, it seemed enormous and it reminded me of the field at the side of Blewburton Hill. Well, I was a big boy now, but it still reminded me of the field by Blewburton Hill. Perhaps that's why I sat and stared at it for so long.

After that first visit it was a long time before I went back, because the first time told me all I needed to know. There was nothing there, nothing and no one. Although I did go back in the end.

The second occasion I found I was somehow not

heading for school, I didn't head for Blewburton Hill, either. I rode out to a village and spent the morning sitting in the church porch, out of the wind, reading the notices about forthcoming marriages and flower rosters and telling myself that in a minute I'd settle down and do my homework, something about *Romeo and Juliet* which we were meant to be reading on account of it is meaningful and relevant and hip.

Not to me, it isn't. I think it is a real mess of a play. Romeo and Juliet are supposed to be easy to identify with because they are about the same age as us, but they are both such dipsticks. You feel they only fall in love because they haven't got anything else to do. Most people in *Hamlet* have jobs, even if it's only being a courtier which is a kind of service industry, but no one in *Romeo and Juliet*, except the nurse and the friar, *does* anything, they just run in a gang and start fights. Nobody say, 'Sorry, guys, can't stop to fight now, I'm late for work.'

But in *Hamlet* everyone is busy-busy-busy, going somewhere, doing something, or spying. If he'd known how, Claudius would have had Elsinore bugged. That's partly Hamlet's problem; he isn't allowed to do what he wants which is to go back to Wittenberg and finish his degree. He's studying philosophy so I suppose he'd have spent a lot of time debating ideas. Now he's got no one to debate with except himself, and the longer he can keep those debates going the longer he can put off killing Claudius. 'I'll stab him now – no, I won't – he's praying. If I kill him now he'll go to heaven. I'll wait until he's full of sin and then send him straight to hell. *Next* time . . .'

You'd think, if he really hated Claudius that much, he wouldn't have waited at all, just run him through the next time they met.

Not that *I* ever thought about killing Claudius. To start with, while Mum was getting to know him, I hardly saw him at all. He was around, someone encroaching on our airspace, but only a blip on my radar, really. There was evidence of him, but we never met. Then one day, at the end of January, four months after the funeral, Mum said, 'Would you like to come out to dinner on Saturday?'

I said, 'Where do you want to go?' before I realized that she hadn't said 'go' she'd said 'come'. The dinner was arranged, what you call a *fait accompli*, and I was being asked to join it.

'Chris invited us,' she said.

'Chris?' I acted dumb.

'You met him at the funeral – he was with David

when he died. He took me to Blewburton—'

Then she remembered how I'd reacted to this or, I suppose, how I hadn't reacted. I'd worked very hard at not reacting.

'Whose idea was it to invite me?'

'Oh, don't be like that.'

'Like what?'

'Suspicious. He's been so kind. He just asked us both to dinner. He wants to meet you.'

'He has met me.'

'Well, hardly, darling . . .'

I don't know how this conversation would have gone on. I went into the garage. I didn't just walk out and leave her talking, the garage has a door straight into the kitchen and I had already opened it to fetch my sports kit which I'd left with my bike. And I noticed something was missing. I don't know how I'd failed to notice before but the light's not wonderful in there. What was missing was three stacks of newspapers tied with string, a box of wine bottles and glass jars, and a bin liner full of flattened tin cans, our bit for the environment.

We have doorstep recycling now; green boxes collected by the council. In those days though we either made visits to the bottle bank or saved up everything and took the whole lot down to the council depot in the car. Mum and I always did that, she making one of her brave stabs at driving, me along to carry the stuff. It's amazing how heavy newspaper is. For weeks I'd been thinking that it was maybe time we made another trip, and waiting for the moment when I could suggest it without seeming heartless, for among the parcels were Dad's last newspapers and his unopened magazines and in the box, his last wine bottle; champagne; wedding anniversary.

We don't go in for keeping mementos, at least we *hadn't*, but every time I passed the glass box, there was the neck of that damned bottle, poking out from among all the others. I knew it by sight. And now it had gone, everything had gone.

'What's happened to the recycling?' I said.

'Oh, we took it down to the depot yesterday afternoon.' She was still in the kitchen so I couldn't see her face, but she sounded unbothered.

'We?'

'Chris.'

'Why'd he want to shift our rubbish?' I said. I meant it. Why would he?

'I just happened to mention it—'

'Why didn't you mention it to *me*? It's never been a

problem before. We never needed any outside help.'

'Don't be silly. I just mentioned that it was piling up and he said, "No problem. We'll take it now." '

'All of it?' There I'd been, afraid to suggest getting rid of it because of The Last Wine Bottle, afraid how she'd take it, and suddenly it's gone, out of the house, bottle and all. And I wasn't the one who'd taken it.

It must have been about that time that I started asking myself what Claudius's plans might be. The radar blip was getting closer. Up to then I hadn't even started to consider what he might be planning and, let's face it, he was hardly the last of the red hot Latin lovers. Look at his courting technique; scattering his predecessor's ashes and toting the garbage.

Dead subtle, in fact. No embarrassing nonsense with red roses and soft music, he was making himself indispensable because he could see that she needed someone indispensable and up to that point I'd thought that she did have someone indispensable – me. I'd thought I was the one who'd help her get over losing Dad, make her laugh, come to life again, carry on doing all the things I'd always done and gradually taking over the things Dad had always done around the place.

Like I said, the man of the house, and don't imagine that I thought my manhood was at risk because some other bloke had taken out the garbage – but couldn't she see how I felt?

No, she couldn't, so I decided to let her know.

I didn't *decide*, it was nothing so, well, decisive, but after supper I didn't clear the plates away, wash up, make coffee. I just got up and said, 'I'm going over to Ozzie's, OK?' Robert Osbourne, who was a good friend, once. I didn't wait for her to say it was OK, or to protest, I just went out saying, 'Back around ten,' and came home at eleven.

Nothing was said about that. Something should have been but it wasn't, so I went out again a couple of nights later and stayed out till after midnight. They say it's the last straw that breaks the camel's back, but it's the first one that really matters. Once I'd started there seemed no reason to stop, and then no way of stopping.

I don't think I'd been asleep. I just suddenly started focussing again, on a horrible sight.

A family had sat down opposite, a proper nuclear family, mum, dad, small boy, small girl and a baby. It was the baby I found I was looking at.

He'd got to that stage where he wasn't quite a baby any more and only his nearest and dearest could possibly think he was cute. (Nicky is fast approaching that phase of his development but I shall remain a true friend.) He wasn't damp and smelly and disgusting, but he was sucking a crocheted blanket. All babies have a sucky-blanket; Nicky does, I did. It still exists. We use it in the cat basket when Mork or Mindy has to go to the vet. It wouldn't have been so bad if he'd been clutching it, but he wasn't. He was leaning back in his seat, half asleep, with his hands by his sides and the blanket was hanging out of his mouth. He looked like a medium producing ectoplasm at a seance, eyes shut, completely out of it, and this horrible soft greyish thing dangling over his chin and dragging on the floor. Every few seconds his jaws moved slightly and the ectoplasm *convulsed*.

If anyone was in a trance it was me, not him. I was beginning to see things, sort of waking dreams. Unlike the others, Terminal 3 goes around corners, it has bays and transepts. It was starting to look to me like a cathedral, as if the walls were curving at the top to meet in a central vault, and although it was brightly lit it seemed shadowy, and as I looked down the length of it I got the impression that the shadows were moving together into huge shapes until everything was dark, then I'd see a sudden bright flash like a magnesium flare, and everything would be light again, and there in front of me was Ectoplasm Baby.

I've had that sensation in bed, falling asleep. It's not called falling asleep, dropping off, for nothing, because you do feel as if you're falling, and wake up with a jolt. But in bed, in the end, you do fall asleep. I couldn't.

Then I saw something I knew I couldn't be seeing, the tiny ten-year-old woman from the Balham flat, Shanti's friend, and I woke up properly before I started seeing ghosts, and went for a walk with my bag, away from the nice family who weren't whining and nagging and squabbling, but just talking and showing each other things in books and being fond of the baby, which was a nice baby, really, even if it did look like something out of the Addams family.

We nearly had a baby once.

Eight

I needed fresh air, or as fresh as it gets at Heathrow, which is not very. At Terminal 2 I remembered seeing a sign to what it called a Spectator Area, so instead of just going outside I went back underground like Hamlet's old mole, and found the right tunnel this time, skimming along the travelator with a trolley. It gives you a spring in your step, that thing, literally. I was bounding along, the trolley zooming ahead. It was the same feeling I get pushing Nicky in his buggy which is a super deluxe GT model.

Unlike the ones in supermarkets, Heathrow trolleys go in a straight line.

Terminal 2 being so cosy, I thought the Spectator Area would be a kind of extension where passengers could pass the time watching aeroplanes. It wasn't. The signs pointed to the Check In exit and round a corner to a scruffy brick building where a notice explained that the lifts weren't working and that there were seventy-two steps to climb. I lugged the bag up them, between bare walls, really tatty. At the top was a long terrace with park benches and then I saw it, the Spectator Area.

It's a viewing platform, right up high, and it was crowded with people, mostly men in anoraks. They had binoculars and telescopes and judging by the bags they had with them they'd come for the day. They weren't spectators, they were plane-spotters, and up there, on that platform, they were in heaven. To the north the airport buildings hid the runway so all I could see was tail fins moving slower than you'd expect, gliding above the rooftops, and then the planes they were attached to leaving the ground. But to the south you could see them landing, a procession of lights in the sky over London, and gradually an aircraft would take shape round the leading light as it lost height and then that miracle moment when that great thing dropped from the air and touched earth.

I don't know how long I stood there, I could have stayed all day, among all those happy guys watching the things they loved, hour after hour, among people who were just as crazy as they were. But I came down in the end and went to look in the gift shop, on the terrace.

It was just a small room crammed with shelves of books about aircraft and airports, cases of model aeroplanes, racks of postcards, and joined on to it was a little snack bar, dead plain, not like the terminal coffee shops. I had a cup of tea there. It's like an island in the middle of the airport, that Spectator Area, nothing to do with the rest of Heathrow at all, *and I had every right to be there*. No one would care how long I stayed. I really felt better, relaxed, then I noticed this woman sidling towards my table, the way people do when they're about to say, 'Is this seat taken?'

'Is this seat taken?' she said.

It wasn't, and nor were any of the others she could have sat in, the place was almost empty; but I'd started to shake my head, 'No' and at the same time nod, 'Yes, you can sit here.' Before I'd finished wobbling I'd begun to wish I'd said, 'Actually, yes, *all* these seats are taken,' because by then I'd seen what she was carrying.

She had a cup of tea in one hand but in the other she had a shopping bag full of books which she stood on the floor. It was one of those boxy, oil-cloth ones with pictures on the sides, we've got one at home with an old Guinness advert on it, but hers was so filthy you couldn't see what the pictures were, and the books

125

were even filthier. I don't mean porn, this was dirt. The dust on them was so thick it had formed a kind of dense furry crust along the tops. It didn't look as if they'd been taken out of the bag for years.

'I've been watching you,' she said.

I wondered if she was an undercover security guard disguised as a bag lady, so I looked at her properly. She wasn't dirty in the way that the bag and the books were dirty, she just didn't look very fresh. Her coat was green, the colour things are that weren't green to start with, but it was the hat that clinched it, one of those woolly knitted things. She might just as well have had *I am out to lunch* embroidered round it.

'I think you are troubled in your mind,' she said.

Well, I was, but not in a way I wanted to discuss with a free-range loony. 'Not really,' I said.

'Your aura has deflated,' the book lady said. 'There's a dim sulphurous flickering.'

She had a nice chatty voice, the sort you don't mind listening to even if it's not saying anything you want to hear. I did not much want to hear any of this.

'I was sent to find you,' she said. By now I realized that if this was true, whoever had sent her was not anyone I had to worry about. 'I think you are in need of directions. I'm so fortunate, I had no directions myself till I came back from Dublin, but now I can pick out people like me and help them.'

She didn't sound Irish. By now she was leaning across the table and those tables are not wide. There was a staleness coming from her, not unwashed, more unaired, and I didn't want to be breathing it in. Now I know what passive smokers object to, but I couldn't move away. There was nothing to stop me, but I couldn't.

Book Lady hadn't stopped talking. She didn't speak fast, she just kept going, the way people do who play wind instruments, until you wonder how they don't burst.

'I was on my own and troubled in my mind, like you, in Dublin Airport,' she said. 'Now, I don't know what I was doing in Dublin Airport, to my knowledge I had no business in the Republic at all, but the Great Genius had arranged for me to be there. I had an appointment with him, though I didn't know it.'

The way she was telling it, she might have been talking about her boss turning up for a business meeting. I had a feeling she meant God.

'Well, Dublin Airport's a marvellous place, the Great Genius himself must have put it in the minds of the architects.' She loomed across the table and said, 'It is perfectly circular.'

She paused to let it sink in and I had this mad picture of a perfectly circular runway, like a ring road for aircraft, and 747s belting round it. Then I realized she meant the terminal, though I didn't know if she was right. It could be triangular in real life.

'Well, I walked and walked in my dark trouble and it seemed to me I was going nowhere, and then I felt a light at my back and the light spoke and said, "When you have walked the circle a hundred times you will see the way ahead." Well, I knew it was the voice of the Great Genius; you do, don't you? And I said, "How many times have I walked the circle already?" and the voice said, "You'll know when you've walked the circle a hundred times," and the light took its hand off my shoulder and I walked on and, what do you think? I saw the sign.'

'What was it?' I said, quickly. She had to stop for breath *sometimes*.

'It was the sign that said, Exit. No, don't laugh. The infinite is often shown to us in the mundane. In my dark trouble I had passed that sign one hundred times without seeing it, but then the darkness left me and I saw it. I knew what I must do, where I had to go. I looked down, and in my hand was an airline ticket to London Heathrow, and I remembered that I'd left there, days before. And I remembered what I'd seen. As my plane took off I looked down and saw the great hexagram, the six-pointed star that is the Sign of Confusion. So I knew I had to go back there and look for others who are troubled in the mind, being under the influence of the dark star, and tell them where they must go.'

She was holding her cup of tea in one hand. Now she banged it down on the table – tea went everywhere – and thumped me on the arm. 'You must go to Dublin and walk the circle one hundred times. The light of the Great Genius will speak to you.' She was smiling now, perhaps my aura was looking healthier. She stood up, picked up her bag of books and took one out.

'Read this,' she said, 'and go to Dublin. Stay away from Heathrow, it is the centre of the world's unrest, drawing souls from all corners of the earth and sending them on their way in sorrow and confusion.'

That's one way of looking at it. I was trying to hold the book without actually touching it, and didn't see her go. This particular volume had a network of cobwebs over it and the dust had got damp and gone into little hard lumps. I put it on the table and opened the cover with one finger to look at the title page:

Ericaceae by R. Dawson. I thought it must be some mind–body–spirit type thing, and Ericaceae were a species of angels, but it was an old gardening book about growing plants in acid soils.

It could have been worse. At least she'd gone away. At least she hadn't looked deep into my eyes and danced about distributing imaginary flowers.

They never get Ophelia right. I've seen two films of *Hamlet* and in both of them she floats about, and has seizures, and floats some more. She wouldn't have done that, that's not how people go mad. I don't know how she'd have behaved in a certain production I didn't see the end of, but the actress playing her was little and big-eyed and looked ready to start floating any minute. But if she'd been really crazy there wouldn't have been any of that song and dance. Like everybody else in the play, she'd have *talked*. She does talk, she gets Laertes and eyeballs him, just like the Book Lady. 'There's fennel for you, and columbines. There's rue for you. And here's some for me. We may call it herb of grace on Sundays. Go to Dublin Airport and walk in circles.'

Poor Laertes; she doesn't recognize her own brother. She was probably still talking when she went into the river, still talking when the air trapped under her skirts stopped her sinking – he must have seen that happen, Shakespeare must. It's not the sort of thing you could make up. Then the cloth got waterlogged and dragged her down, still talking.

Someone he knew, perhaps, who drowned in the Avon or the Thames.

The pub in Terminal 2 is called the Shakespeare, that is, the bar that is faked up to look like a pub, and there used to be a Shakespeare Tavern out near the ring road. The building's still there but some chain got hold of it and tore out all the fittings, filled it up with trendy rubbish and renamed it Mywitz End, presumably so cretins can call up their friends on the mobe and say, 'I'm at my wit's end.'

When it was still a pub, they did good food. Mum and I used to walk up there for dinner sometimes, and get a cab home – when Dad was away. When we all went out together we usually went to Rossini's, an Italian restaurant off the High Street, not very adventurous but the cooking was good. And Dad ate in so many different places he said it was nice to have something *certain* to come back to. I can imagine what he'd have said about Mywitz End.

I wondered what Chris Hague's idea of a dinner

date involved and I wondered if I was going to find out. I'd said I would go along, but that had been on the Monday and the Occasion was scheduled for Saturday. In between I'd been perfecting the storming-out-and-coming-home-late routine and it would finish the week off satisfactorily if I failed to show at the appointed hour. It was a time when Adam and I were still playing our game about the insurance money, so I was not only curious but as suspicious as Mum thought I was. I decided I'd go.

I asked her where we were going but she said she didn't know. Chris would call for us at 7.30.

'Does he drink and drive, then?' I said nastily, but she said we were taking taxis.

'Can't we get a bus in?'

'I don't think we're eating in town,' which gave me the idea that somewhere like Rossini's wasn't good enough for Hague. This didn't really fit the theory that he was after our money, unless he was prepared to lay out a lot in the hope of big returns. I could imagine the headlines after the police tracked him down: HIGH LIFE CONMAN PREYED ON WIDOW.

Thinking about it made me realize that I didn't know a thing about him, his job, his age, where he lived, whether he had a family. I assumed he didn't have a wife.

You could ask the same questions about Hamlet's Claudius, because we don't know anything about him, either. Claudius poisoned a man with a grown-up son. Whatever the gravedigger says, you can't think of Hamlet as a man of thirty, but he must be about twenty when the play starts. People went to Uni much earlier in those days, but he's not a kid. What had Claudius been up to all those years while Hamlet was growing up? Had he always had his eye on the crown? Had he always had the hots for Gertrude? Why did he wait for so long before making a move? Ah – maybe he was waiting until Hamlet was well and truly out of the way in Wittenberg. But even if that's the answer, what had he been doing? Why hadn't he got married and had a family? Perhaps he was married and one of those things we never find out about is a conveniently dead wife, Hamlet's auntie. Fell out of a window at just the right moment.

So I was curious enough to go along with the dinner invite. Come Saturday evening I showered and made myself presentable, but no more presentable than I would have done for Rossini's. Shoes, not trainers, but no tie. I even polished the shoes.

Then Mum came down. She'd had her hair cut during the week but I hadn't associated it with the Occasion because she has it done every six weeks or so anyway, but the first thing I noticed was her earrings. She hadn't done herself up specially, but there was a sort of *sheen* about her; no new clothes but everything smooth and gleaming, shoes, stockings, skirt, top, make-up – *make-up*. She hadn't even been wearing lipstick lately – then the hairstyle and the earrings. The earrings *were* new. Had she bought them specially? Had he bought them for her? They weren't embarrassingly flash, not diamonds or anything, but she usually wears studs.

I didn't say anything. I was getting good at that. Well, what I did say was, 'Will I do?' implying that I must look a bit drab alongside and hoped she'd take the hint, but she just said, 'Of course you'll do,' and went and waited in the living room and wouldn't let Mindy sit on her lap. Mindy is black and white and only sheds the white hairs, or so it seems, making a special effort for people who are dressed in black, but Mum never minded about that kind of thing before.

Mindy went and sat on her wrap which was hanging over the back of the sofa and is also black. Mum didn't notice and I didn't say anything.

The cab arrived dead on 7.30. Out we traipsed and there was Hague doing his door-opening act. I went round the back and got in on the off-side so that Mum was sitting between us. I got the impression that she was starting to *snuggle* so I said, 'Don't forget to fasten your seatbelt,' and pointed to the sign, so we all had to get up and find the attachments, and fumble. That made everything a bit less smooth, heh–heh.

Then the cab got going and Hague leaned across and said, 'I don't suppose you remember me – we met only very briefly.'

'I remember,' I said, as if something vile had happened at the time which had made it impossible for me to forget.

For some reason this killed the conversation stone dead. I hadn't meant it to but I wasn't sorry. It's bad enough trying to talk to someone sitting alongside you, let alone someone you don't much want to speak to and particularly if you're having to talk *across* somebody else. I wondered how I'd done it so that I could do it again. Was it what I'd said or the way I'd said it?

I looked out of the window and left Hague to realize his big mistake in coming to fetch us instead of letting us meet him at the restaurant, but after a bit I began to see that it would have just been rude to leave us to make our own way there. At first I wondered why he hadn't driven over himself, but there was a faint scent of whisky in the air which made me suspect that he'd been building up his nerve. I *hated* to admit that he wouldn't drink and drive. It was a thirty-minute trip right out into the country which starts sharpish at the ring road, to one of those country-house places that have been turned into restaurants or hotels; both in this case. Adlington Manor Hotel.

It was a really nice place; you couldn't go there in a shell suit but it wasn't so formal that anyone just tidy would feel out of place, and the staff were friendly.

And they knew *him*.

'Good evening, Mr Hague,' said the girl at Reception.

Brings all his women here, I thought sardonically; then I realized that he was *staying* there.

'Are you staying here?' I said.

'Just overnight,' he said. 'I live in Leeds.'

The Louse from Leeds, I thought, Adam-like.

'Did you stay here when you went to Blewburton?'

'*Where?*'

He wasn't fooling. The name of the place hadn't meant anything to him.

'When you took Mum out to scatter the ashes.'

He looked uncomfortable. Good. 'I was just driving back from London, that time.'

'What about the other time — times?'

'*Russell.*' Mum was beginning to twitter, looking a little less glossy. 'Don't be so aggressive.'

I wasn't doing it on purpose, but it wasn't the moment or the place for that kind of conversation. We were still cluttering up Reception and there was a couple alongside trying to check in and a family party backing up behind us.

'A friend recommended it,' Hague said. 'Look, shall we go straight to the table or would you like a drink first? Sarah?'

Who said you could call her Sarah? I thought. Well, she had, obviously and, obviously, if she called him Chris he wouldn't be calling her Mrs Jagger, but it sounded odd.

'Oh, let's sit down and we can have a drink while we order.' Mum sounded a little desperate already, afraid I was going to make a scene. I *wasn't*, not intentionally at any rate, but what did she expect? What did she think I expected? What was I meant to say to this person I didn't know, who'd got to know her over my head? If she'd ever talked about him it would have been easier. This half-formal business made it as difficult as it could be. Why hadn't she asked him round to ours for a meal? Perhaps she had, and he hadn't wanted to meet me on my home turf. I wouldn't have wanted to meet him on his. This Adlington Manor Hotel was neutral territory.

They gave us a table in a bay window but you couldn't make out what lay beyond it except for an urn on the terrace outside. In the dark distance I could see the power station lights and knew that Blewburton Hill was out there somewhere.

'What do you drink, Russell?' Hague asked me when the waiter showed up. He was trying to say, 'What are you allowed to drink?' but being tactful. It would have been more tactful just to let me order what I wanted but he might have been afraid I'd ask for a double brandy, or absinthe, or meths.

'We usually have wine,' I said meaningly, to remind him that 'we' didn't include him.

He took the hint and ordered a bottle of red, from way down the list, I noted, and we all studied our menus.

They were pricy. I guessed the whole place was pricy. This was an expensive weekend, for him, putting up at Adlington Manor just so he could take us to dinner.

Mind you, he needn't have done. He could have stayed at a B&B and we'd never have known.

It was a very good dinner. Even the starter was so good it gave us something to talk about and I knew that we were in the presence of a serious foodie. I don't mean that he was greedy but he was interested in what he ate and liked cooking. He and Mum were talking about ways of cooking fish which was a laugh, if he did but know it. He knows now.

I looked up and saw aircraft lights climb diagonally across the black window pane. Too late for Concorde. Now and again one of them said something to try and make me join in the conversation, but I made do with yes and no and thanks, when somebody passed me something. It was like being with two strangers, not one. She wasn't putting on an act or anything, but everything they said sounded like they were making an effort. Which they were. Hague talked a bit about work but I still couldn't make out what it was he actually did, and I thought of that part in *Pretty Woman* where Julia Roberts asks Richard Gere what he does for a living and says something like, 'But you don't *make* anything?'

That sounded very like Hague's line of work. He didn't *make* anything.

'What are your plans?' Hague said, suddenly, in the middle of the main course. Mine was something with ducks in it. His was venison.

'Plans about what?' I said.

'After school – University.'

I thought of saying that I was planning to be a rent boy, another conversation stopper, but even I could see that it wasn't a bright idea, just then, so I said I hadn't got as far as making plans. I'd think about that after GCSE.

It was a lie. I'd once been planning like mad, but in private, because I knew that in the end the future would be GCSE, then A levels, then Mod Lang at Uni – I fancied Bristol – then travel, anywhere, doing anything, putting the Mod Lang to good use. The reason I'd never mentioned these perfectly respectable ideas was because I could imagine how Mum would react to *two* of us jetting around the world.

Given the way things were turning out, though, rent boy might quite possibly be the only option.

'I might join the RAF,' I said. 'Only joking,' I added, hastily, but the damage was done. I'd *reminded* her. Of aeroplanes. Aeroplanes = death. She didn't want to think of that so she started talking very hard and fast about nothing – I think that's literally true. I can't remember a word of it. It seemed to make about as much sense as Lucky's speech in *Waiting for Godot*.

Hague began to look awkward. I was picking up signals. They didn't know each other well enough yet to share jokes or talk easily about nothing in particular, or talk seriously about things that mattered. It had been a mistake, coming here, bringing me along. The evening wasn't quite a disaster, it wasn't dramatic enough for that, but it wasn't turning out well. Mainly, if we went on like this, signals would be all I would get. I wasn't learning anything.

'How well did you know Dad?' I said. Ooh, it did go quiet.

'I didn't know him,' Hague said, at last. Mum had jumped so much her earrings were still trembling, but Hague seemed relieved. 'We were taxiing when it happened.'

'You hadn't met before?'

'*Russell—*'

'Only when we boarded. I'd sat down first in the aisle seat, then I got up to let him in, and we rearranged our stuff in the overhead locker.'

'What did you say to each other?'

'I can't remember, the usual gripes about seat width and leg room and rough flying weather. We were just being polite. We never got the chance to be more than that.'

He stopped. I didn't need to make him go on. The next time he'd looked at the man in the seat beside him he had collapsed over his laptop. Two complete strangers who just happened to be sitting next to each other and now, here was one stranger talking to the other stranger's widow and orphan; not just talking, wining and dining them. This man had no more in common with Mum than he'd had with Dad. He'd done the decent thing to Dad because he was too decent not to, but what was he doing now?

I looked across the table at him and Mum, who were closer to one another than they were to me – an accident, I'm sure. Mum was nervously gripping her napkin and I saw her wedding ring with the candlelight on it, and that's when the line about funeral baked meats occurred to me. The remains of our main course were still on the plates – the waiter was just advancing to clear them away as it happened – and some words crossed my mind: *funeral baked meats* and *marriage tables*.

I could see those funeral baked meats, the remains of the meal, picked over like my duck's legs, and the skin off whatever Mum had been eating, cold juices, congealed sauce, limp vegetables.

I didn't know where the line came from then, but I looked it up in the dictionary of quotations at school; *Hamlet Act I Scene 2*.

I'd never read *Hamlet*, never seen it, but I got it out of the library and I looked up the line. In context it was even worse.

Horatio: My lord, I came to see your father's funeral.
Hamlet: I prithee do not mock me, fellow student.
I think it was to see my mother's wedding.
Horatio: Indeed, my lord, it followed hard upon.
Hamlet: Thrift, thrift, Horatio. The funeral baked meats
Did coldly furnish forth the marriage tables.

Then I sat down and read the play. Father's funeral, mother's wedding. Suddenly it all fell into place. That was the moment, there in the school library, when Christopher Hague became Claudius.

Nine

So up and down Departures I went all night, lifts, escalators, studying the monitors, looking in shops until the shutters came down, and, later on went up again, a drink here, a coffee there, sleepwalking, more or less. But whenever I found a quiet spot and sat down and waited to go to sleep, I couldn't. I picked up newspapers; read, re-read pages of the book, which is the surest way to make your eyes close, but when they did close and there came a few seconds of the falling sensation in the dark, I'd wake up again with that jolt. Once I thought I'd gone back in time and Ectoplasm Baby was sitting in front of me, but it was only a coat slung over the back of a seat. Ectoplasm Baby and his family were airborne by now, I guessed. Probably everyone I'd seen was airborne, going somewhere.

Then I did see someone I'd seen before, or thought I'd seen before. Crossing the concourse was the tiny ten-year-old woman from Shanti's flat. There was no doubt at all about it this time, it was her, no mistaking the very black hair, or the tinyness. I'd been exaggerating that first time I saw her, even though she'd been getting smaller and smaller in my imagination until she was about three feet tall.

But seeing her now, she couldn't have been much more than five feet and she wasn't just short, everything about her was a bit smaller than you'd expect it to be, as if she'd been designed as a scale model, and perfect in that surprising way that scale models are. You admire them even while you wonder why anyone had bothered to do it.

Not that tiny-woman wasn't worth the bother. At that moment she was definitely worth the bother. I stood up and went over to where I'd intercept her flight path and just as I was starting to panic over what to say to her she stopped and smiled *up* and said, 'How can I help you?'

I took it in then. The tiny skirt and jacket were a uniform. She worked there. She was on duty. She wasn't a bit alarmed at strange hairy blokes flagging her down; that was what she was there for.

I said, 'Do you remember me?'

'I'm sorry?' She must have thought I was a lost

passenger she'd dealt with who'd got lost all over again. Of course she didn't remember me, she'd hardly seen me in those few seconds crossing the flat to get out of range before the shit hit the fan. I wouldn't have had time to remember her, either, if she hadn't been so, well, memorable.

I said, 'We've met before – at your flat. On Monday.' She still looked blank. Perhaps she was starting to feel uneasy; there are as many loonies wandering around Heathrow as there are any other place, don't I know it. More, even. 'I was with Shanti's brother. Adam.'

Light dawned.

'Oh,' she said. Then she *beamed*. 'Are you Russell or Curtis?' She had a tiny accent too, not quite English. 'No, you must be Russell.'

'I'm Russell.'

'Well, Russell, this is quite extraordinary.' It was a surprise, hearing her talk so very grown-up. 'I have something of yours.'

This was even more of a surprise, quite extraordinary, as she'd said. Here was someone I didn't know who claimed she had something of mine. And she seemed to expect me to know what it was.

'Something of mine?'

'You didn't know you'd lost it?'

'What is it?'

'An envelope. It had your name on it.'

All I could think of was the envelope with the letter from McPherson that I'd torn up and finally lost in a wayside litter bin. I could see it magically reassembling itself.

'It hadn't been opened,' she said. Then she went on, 'After you'd gone I found it on the floor – a long while after you'd gone, when I came home from work. It had slipped under the telephone table. It just said *Russell* on the front. I didn't know where you had all gone, I didn't even know who you all were, and Shanti was out. So I opened it to see if there was an address.'

'What was in it?'

'Just a note saying *I expect you can make use of this –* and fifty pounds.'

'Fifty pounds?' I didn't believe I was hearing this. 'Who was the note from?'

'It said, *Chris,*' she said. 'If only I'd known I should meet you here – but how could I? Did you not know you had it?'

He must have slipped it into one of my pockets when he went to work. I remembered then that he'd asked me which jacket I'd be taking and I'd told him, thinking, *What business is it of yours?* and even considering wearing something different just to spite him. As it turned out I might just as well have. It would only have been me who was spited, anyway.

If only I'd known.

'I'm afraid I haven't got it on me,' she said. 'At first we thought you'd come back for it. Then, on Tuesday, when Shanti's mother rang, looking for Adam . . . well, we didn't know where you were.'

I kept thinking, *Fifty pounds*. Poor old Claudius, doing something Dad-like for once, and I'd blown it.

'This is none of my business, Russell,' she said, 'but I'm sure you're not meant to be here. Do you need the money?'

Not as much as I *had* needed it, but— 'I do,' I said, wistfully.

'I can get you fifty pounds if you don't mind waiting a little – and I'll keep yours in exchange. I'm just coming off shift.'

'Oh, yes, please.' I felt alive again, not only at the prospect of the fifty pounds but just having had a proper conversation with someone. She told me to wait, said she'd be back in about twenty minutes. I went and sat down again.

Then I started fretting; suppose she got in touch with someone; Mum and Claudius might be back by now. Adam's family and the Rules knew I was still out there somewhere. Suppose she told Shanti, the police? Was I a Missing Person?

I took my bag and went and looked in the bookshop on the next level, one eye on the stock, one eye on the concourse, watching for her to come back and to see who she came with. The assistant had *both* eyes on me, not surprisingly.

At last I saw tiny-woman returning. I didn't know where she'd come from − you never do see where people are coming from in a place like that. But she was alone − as far as I could tell. In my paranoid state I was imagining cops peering out of concealed apertures. I came out of the shop before she'd got to where we'd met so she wouldn't think I'd been in hiding.

'Would you like a coffee?' she said. I guessed we were going to have a quiet talk, but I couldn't refuse. She had the cash.

'Let me get it,' I said, and she did. We went to the coffee shop and sat down.

'What's your name?' I said. It was a bit abrupt but I couldn't call her Tiny-Ten-Year-Old-Woman to her face.

'Xaviera,' she said, 'spelled with an X.' X is the sign of a good woman, I thought. She must be the one who owned all those French and Spanish books in the flat.

'I'm not sure I should be doing this,' Xaviera said, handing me the notes. 'Are you running away?'

Just like that, straight out. But she'd given me the money.

'How much do you know?' I said.

'Only that you and your friends were supposed to be going on a school visit and came to London instead. We found out – we worked it out – when Shanti's mother rang up. What is going on? Do your parents know where you are? No, I don't suppose they do.'

If she went on like this she was going to have answered all the questions herself. I cut in.

'Not unless Adam's spilled the beans. We got banned from going on the trip and decided to go to London instead because we didn't want anyone to know.'

'But you must have known they'd find out.'

'Just needed a bit of time,' I said, 'Adam thought we could sleep at Shanti's. We were going to go home on Friday. Then that pig, what's his name, Tim—'

'He is not a pig,' Xaviera said, 'he is a doctor.'

'He behaved like a pig.' A *doctor*. And we'd thought he was a pimp. 'The way he talked to Shanti—'

'He was protecting her.'

'From *us*?' What a thought . . .

'From consequences. He remembered what happened last time Adam came to stay.'

'Do you?'

'Remember? No, I didn't know Shanti then, but he did. Russell, can you imagine what it was like for Shanti? The police turning up in the middle of the night, and all the trouble afterwards. It was in the papers. She was still a student . . . for all Tim knew she would have to face something like that again. He knows how soft-hearted she is, she would have given in—'

'She had given in.'

'Yes, and he knows if he had given her the chance she would have talked him round. So he put his foot down.'

'He talked like he owned her.'

'He doesn't. He's not like that. He doesn't even live with us, but he could see what would have happened. And it did. Curtis got arrested. Tim was just making sure it didn't involve Shanti.'

'Curt told his parents, and they told Adam's.'

'And yours?'

'They've been in France. They'll be home today – tomorrow.' I looked at my watch. It was 7.30 a.m. Thursday. 'Today.'

'So what are you going to do?'

'What are *you* going to do?'

'I?' I'd have said me. Foreigners always seem to speak better English than we do.

'Are you going to report me?'

'Have you broken the law?'

Apart from Possession, which I wasn't doing at that moment, I hadn't. And my very casual approach to attending school. That's illegal, I suppose.

'No – I don't think so,' I added cautiously.

'If your parents don't know yet what has happened you are not even a missing person.' It dawned on me that she was reassuring herself, not me. 'Are you going to go home now?'

'Not this minute,' I said. I looked at my watch again. 7.33. 'We were all going to go home Friday afternoon anyway.' The coach from Cumbria was due back at school at 4.30 p.m.

'You're going home this afternoon?'

'No, tomorrow, Friday.'

'Russell, it is Friday.' She was looking at me very hard, the way the book lady had. My aura must be on the blink again.

'It can't be.'

'It is.' She showed me her watch, which had the date on: 25 February.

I'd lost a whole day. Where? In Terminal 4? On the viewing platform? Somewhere in a tunnel? What had I been doing?

'Why not go home now, right away? The trains are running.' She sounded really urgent.

I wouldn't even need to get a train. I could catch a coach direct from the Central Bus Station. I could afford it now.

That wasn't all I could afford, now. A thought, an idea, started to form but I terminated it in case Xaviera had some kind of access to my mental processes, through the eyes, perhaps. She had.

'But you *are* going to go home, aren't you?' she said. 'You can't stay away for ever.' But people do, she must have known that. 'Are you afraid of what will happen when your parents find out what's been going on?'

Was I? What was it I'd been trying to avoid all week? Since last Friday, in fact. Compared to Hamlet I had nothing to worry about. Claudius wasn't going to have me sent on a mission out of the country in the company of two hatchet men and have me murdered. I suppose I was really afraid of their disappointment, or resentment – the trip to France ruined because they wouldn't have been able to go. That letter from McPherson had requested (hah!) an interview on . . . I hadn't read that far. Adam had said his was for Tuesday, maybe mine was too. No doubt by now there would have been other letters which hadn't been intercepted, letters received by the Holders and the Rules, and one lying on the mat waiting for Mr and Mrs Hague – no, Mrs X would have found it by now and added it to the pile on the working surface when she came to feed the cats.

All week I'd been telling myself I could face anything – when I was ready to – but now I knew I couldn't. I hadn't got ready, hadn't been getting ready. I'd been in Limbo.

'Are you afraid of what will happen when your parents find out what's been going on?'

'No,' I said. I was calculating whether I could get back and destroy the second letter and take off again before they did get home. I could, easily.

No, I couldn't. It wasn't Thursday, it was Friday. Where had I *been*?

Xaviera was looking a bit disheartened. I knew that look. I saw it on so many faces, people who knew they weren't making any headway with me. She was already wishing that she hadn't given me the fifty pounds, I could tell. I was grateful, I was trying to show it, but of course I was also trying not to show anything else.

'I ought to be going home,' she said, tiredly.

'Are you going to tell anyone you've seen me?'

'I ought to tell Shanti about the money. But it won't matter, will it, if you're going home too?'

'No,' I said. That 'no' covered a lot of things, and she knew it. 'Thanks for the money. I really appreciate that.'

'Don't do anything silly, will you?'

She meant anything criminal, because now she was an accessory before the fact.

She got up and went. I watched her disappear down the steps without looking back, the way I'd watched Adam on the escalator. Then I looked over the railing and saw her, tiny-tiny-tiny, stride down the concourse and disappear. She'd given up. She didn't know what to say to me and she was feeling guilty – what silly, criminal thing did she think I was going to do with the fifty quid? Asking herself how she would feel if I disappeared altogether on the proceeds and left her blaming herself. She was involved, now, no longer an innocent bystander; not even an accessory, an accomplice.

I got another coffee. I was rich. Now I could start thinking about things I hadn't dared to think about before.

Suppose I didn't go home? How much grief would it really cause? Something that no one seems to notice in *Hamlet* is that Claudius has only himself to blame for what happens. I don't mean the murder, which he committed, no question; but right at the beginning of the play Hamlet wants to go back to Wittenberg, it's Claudius who persuades him to stay. Hamlet says he'll stay for Gertrude's sake, as a snub to Claudius, so that Claudius will know that Hamlet doesn't care what he wants. Why *did* he want him to stay? Seeing the mood Hamlet's in (even before the Ghost tells him about the murder) you'd think he'd want him out of the way. He certainly wants him out of the way for good after the Polonius business. He must have cursed himself for not letting Hamlet go back to Wittenberg.

After the dinner at Adlington Manor our Claudius began to show up more often. He didn't try to keep me out of the way, he kept out of mine. Mum met him in London or he took her out for the day. They were either being very careful or very tactful. She was always home before I came back from school.

That was a laugh, really, because mostly I wasn't at school. I was staying out until it was officially time to come home. If I ever did get back first I went round to see Mrs X. I wished I was indispensable, there to do things for Mrs X, like fetch and carry, before the baby was born, and help out with things afterwards, but she had Mr X. He is a proper story-book husband – no, more a reading-scheme husband – who comes home at about the same time every night and does the shopping. When Nicky was born he did the night feeds and changed nappies and helped with the cooking.

I didn't feel squeezed out by him, I mean, I didn't have any rights there anyway, but it just seemed to make what was happening at home worse, where I really was being squeezed out – not squeezed, exactly, just not having a proper place any more. I thought a lot about the baby, about the baby *we* didn't have, and how different it would have been if there were two of us, shoulder to shoulder against the world, although most people with little brothers and sisters don't seem to feel like that about them. Curt doesn't, and Adam just *used* his sisters.

I never even knew what ours would have been. I was ten. Didn't realize then that you could tell. Didn't know what questions to ask. Little Bro or Little Sis would be about six by now. Mum and Dad said they would try again, but nothing happened. Perhaps that's why I liked being around Mrs X so much.

Never mind the family that Claudius doesn't have, what about Hamlet? I know people died like flies in those days but – *had* there been any brothers and sisters? It's the same in *Macbeth*. Lady M says she's had children, 'Given suck', she says, but there aren't any little Macbeths around. The truth is, they'd just have got in the way – of the play, I mean, cluttering up the action. Apart from the lords and ladies and people like Osric, there is no one in *Hamlet* who doesn't need to be there. Shakespeare was writing for bums-on-seats, for punters who'd probably seen a public execution in the morning, watched a bear-baiting after lunch, and were taking in a play before they went on to the brothel next door, not people who were going to sit there and pick over every line or write pages of notes about single words. Or people like me who were going to think and think about it afterwards and wonder what might have happened if things had turned out differently, imagining themselves part of it all.

Once I'd started thinking of Hague as Claudius I couldn't help casting myself as Hamlet. Sitting there in Terminal 2 after Xaviera had gone I knew that Hamlet and I didn't have much in common really, except Gertrude. Hague was no wicked uncle, not a wicked anything. He was just the man Mum had wanted to marry.

How soon did I know? I mean, actually *know* as opposed to being suspicious and making jokes about it with Adam. I can see now why I made the jokes, as if refusing to take the idea seriously would prevent it from becoming reality.

It was about a year after Dad died – what am I saying? It was exactly eleven months and three weeks – one of those days when I came home before she did. I wasn't round at Mrs X's, she'd taken Nicky to the clinic.

When Mum came in with that shining look I didn't ask where she'd been. I said, 'What do you do?'

She looked so taken aback. 'What do you mean?'

'Like I said, what do you do? What do you do when you're out with him? Where do you go?'

'Why do you ask now?' The shine was going dim.

'Because I didn't ask before.'

'We just go and have lunch; sometimes we go for walks.'

'Where?'

'In London. We only meet when he's in London.'

'What about next Wednesday?'

She knew what I meant. Next Wednesday it would

be exactly a year since Dad died. I don't know if they'd been planning anything but when Wednesday came round she didn't go anywhere. I didn't ask if we were going to mark the date, like maybe go up to Blewburton Hill, and we didn't, but early in the evening when she went down to the pillar box to catch the last post, I went into her room, that had been hers and Dad's, and looked around.

When things had started to settle down, about a fortnight after the funeral, she and Gran had sorted out all his clothes and shoes and stuff, and taken them to Oxfam in town. I knew there was nothing like that left, but now there was nothing at all. Everything had gone, his electric shaver, his spare glasses, the laptop that Claudius had brought home himself, the filofax and notebooks and letters that he'd kept in the cabinet on his side of the bed. His travelling alarm clock was missing, the little green leather-covered wind-up one that he'd had from when he was a student, the computer disks, the books.

She must have been shifting it out of the house bit by bit so that I wouldn't notice, and I hadn't noticed. I'd just assumed that it was all still there. I didn't know if she'd done it to spare my feelings or if she hadn't thought about my feelings at all. Not even considered that I had any.

I'm not sure that she does realize. I know how that feels, everyone does. When you're a little kid you don't take it in that people are just like you; they're kind of soft furnishings that move about, part of the scenery. It's a long while before you understand that you are part of *their* scenery. That's why little kids are so horrible to each other. They don't know how it feels because they don't know that other people do feel. Some big kids too. Adam for instance. And Mum; and Gertrude. (Less than two months after the King was dead Gertrude married his brother, his murderer.)

It was six weeks after the anniversary that Mum asked me what I thought of Claudius. 'What do you think of Chris?'

I said I didn't think about him.

'But do you like him?'

'He's all right.'

What else could I say? I didn't know him, they'd seen to that, between them, being so tactful. Or sneaky. The whole thing was carried on out of sight, out of hearing. There weren't even any phone calls when I was around which is why I eavesdropped so much on calls from other people, because I was sure there ought

161

to be. Conspicuous by his absence, Claudius was, so when she said coyly, 'What would you say if I told you I was thinking of marrying again?' it didn't come as a shock, but it was a surprise.

'Who to?' I said, and then when she tried to come up with an answer I said, 'Bit soon, isn't it?'

'Some people find it very hard to be alone,' she said.

'You're not alone.'

'Oh, darling, I know I've got you—'

'And Granny and Grandad. What does Granny think?'

But, as I said, it was no good expecting her to wonder what somebody else thought, except about curtains and plumbers.

'I wouldn't have told her before I told you.'

Believe that if you like. 'You're *telling* me, then.'

'I won't do anything unless—'

'Yes you will,' I said, and went out. It didn't matter what I wanted, she'd go right ahead and do it.

And a month after that she did do it. They did it.

That was when Claudius tried to have a heart to heart, or man to man, or eyeball to eyeball. 'I'm not trying to take your father's place.'

'You couldn't,' I said.

'Try not to resent me too much,' was all he said. If

he'd been going to say anything else he gave up and never tried again.

They got married in London, that Town Hall place like a museum on Marylebone Road. Often when the coach goes by you look out and see a wedding party on the steps, getting ready to go in and do it, or poncing about being photographed afterwards.

It was just about the most embarrassing thing I can remember, everyone was embarrassed; me, Granny, Grandad, Mum's oldest friend Janice from school, who I'd never even seen before, and Claudius. (Who had no one on his side. Murdered them all, I told myself.) Everyone except Mum. Brides are meant to be radiant. I suppose that's what she was, in a cream silk suit with freesias. Then we went and had lunch in some hotel and then we went home. There was no honeymoon. Well, I didn't imagine they'd waited.

Claudius didn't move in right away. He was still trying to sell his flat in Leeds, but Mum was kind of feathering a nest for him. Well, feather me out, I thought. I can take a hint.

It was about then that I started spending more time up on Blewburton Hill, just in case my father's ghost showed up perhaps, and told me what I was hoping to hear.

Ten

I looked in the newsagent's, at the papers. It was definitely Friday, 25 February. I couldn't put off the future any longer, it had overtaken me, leapfrogging over Thursday, into the present. Squaring my shoulders I went and did the ablutions, changed, shaved, scrubbed my teeth like I was cleaning the loo, which is just what it felt like, to be honest.

Not even a good wash could make me look less like a vampire, sort of yellowish, gaunt and red-eyed. I might well have been sleeping in a coffin for the last four days, or a 747 for one night. Still, even Dracula is always immaculate. Someone ought to do a kind of revisionist movie, *The Private Life of Dracula*, where we see what he's up to when he's not puncturing jugulars; Dracula shaving, Dracula at the washing machine, Dracula doing the ironing. That's what I looked like, a vampire with access to modern amenities.

But going out through Arrivals, I didn't seem out of place. People were coming through from the overnight long-hauls. Everyone looked like the living dead. Those who were used to it didn't seem to notice but the rest were having trouble steering. One of them yawned, a huge jaw-cracking yawn. It's catching. In seconds everyone was yawning, me included. In the tunnel, leaning against my trolley on the travelator, I started to feel sleepy. Sleepy. At last, now I didn't need to sleep, it was finally kicking in.

So I didn't hang about when we got to the Underground concourse, but gathered speed in the direction of Terminal 1, bright (red) eyed and bushy-tailed. I belonged. I had a right to be here. I was finally going somewhere. Because I'd done one thing right, from the very beginning, although I hadn't planned it that way. I had my passport with me. This wasn't a miraculous coincidence, either. I happen to keep it in my wallet. The real miracle was that I hadn't left the wallet on the floor of Xaviera's flat.

Terminal 1's a no-nonsense kind of place, more like a railway station. I went straight to the Aer Lingus desk and asked the price of a single to Dublin.

'£105,' said the Aer Lingus lady, then, seeing my

expression, no doubt, added, 'but it's cheaper to buy a return.'

'How much cheaper?'

'A return costs £65,' she said. There must be some logic in this. Perhaps the Irish just want to make sure people go away again. I wasn't arguing, though. I paid up.

It wasn't until I'd asked that I began to wonder if they'd sell me a ticket anyway. Would they ask for ID, demand to know my age, want evidence of parental consent? I didn't know if it was even legal for me to leave the country at my age. I can probably join the army and go and get killed. I can legally screw someone of the opposite sex – marry them even – but can I buy an airline ticket?

Maybe suffering had aged me. Ms Aer Lingus just saw another passenger, clattered on her computer and came up with a flight at 11.45. When money changed hands, so did the ticket.

The Aer Lingus woman was telling me something about departure gates and checking-in times, but I hardly heard. All I knew was that I was going and that I'd never had any intention of returning home. True, I'd been thinking all week about *not* being at Heathrow any more, after Friday, but beyond that had been a dark grey mist. I wasn't going to Dublin to seek enlightenment by walking one hundred times around the airport terminal, but the book lady had put the place into my head. I could never have got this far, ticket in hand, if I'd had to make up my mind where to go. My mind hadn't been made up in a long while, the way a bed doesn't get made up. As Book Lady said, I'd needed directions, and she'd given them to me.

Should I check in the bag? I had hours to go. I went and sat down on one of the rows of seats near the gates. There was plenty of room. I could do what I liked, now, with that ticket in my pocket. I was free. I got an old newspaper out of a bin, put it under my feet on the next seat − one has one's standards − and stretched out, and finally went to sleep.

If I dreamed I don't remember it, except right at the end when I heard someone calling me and I started to get out of bed. I was dreaming *that* because when I woke up properly I wasn't getting out of bed, I was still draped over the seats in Terminal 1 and somebody *was* calling me.

It was the PA system. 'If Mr Russell Jagger is in Departures will he please go to the Airport Information desk—'

I looked at my watch, it was half past twelve. I'd missed the flight. Why hadn't they called me before? I hadn't even checked in, that's why. So why were they bothering to call me now? Perhaps the flight had been delayed.

I was thinking all this while I was sitting up. I didn't feel at all refreshed after my long sleep. I felt as if I'd been quietly dying and someone had resuscitated me. Death warmed up, exactly like that. But I grabbed the bag and did the Headless Chicken round the concourse, looking for the Information Desk. There were two or three people standing by it and one of them was Claudius.

I started to skid round and take off again but he'd seen me before I saw him and somehow he was in front of me before I'd finished turning round.

'Don't start a fight,' he said. 'For all we know they could be filming us. Or do you want to be the latest docu-soap discovery?'

I just dropped the bag and said, 'How did you know I was here?'

'Luck,' he said. 'I was going to work my way round the terminals.'

'No, how did you know I was at Heathrow?'

'Someone rang us.'

Shanti? Adam's mother? Curt's mother? Xaviera? 'Who?'

'A friend of your friend's sister, I think.' Xaviera. Of course. 'I didn't take the call, Sarah did. Need I say more?'

'Is she here?'

'No, she's at home, having nineteen nervous breakdowns. Do me a favour, Russ. Come back with me?'

'What's the point?' If I left the bag I could outrun him, easily.

'What's the alternative?' That was the point. I had twenty quid and a useless airline ticket. 'At least let's talk.'

I didn't know how to talk to Claudius, having spent fifteen months making sure I didn't find out how to. 'Yes, all right.' No one was taking any notice of us but there *could* have been a television crew lurking with a long-distance lens. Let him do the talking. I could always lose him later, discreetly.

Claudius took out his mobe and hit the recall button. 'Do you want to speak to her?'

'Not now.'

She must have been sitting by the phone, it was answered instantly. 'Yes,' Claudius said. 'Yes, he's here.

Terminal 1. No, not at the moment. No, he's fine. Give us a couple of hours . . . something to eat . . . Yes. Bye bye.

'You do want something to eat?' he said, putting the phone away.

For some reason I thought of Adlington Manor; funeral baked meats. My stomach elbowed me in the ribs. 'Not really.'

'Drink?'

'No.' Mainly I wanted to go to sleep again. Claudius could talk and I could do what I was really good at; take no notice.

'Well, I do. You can have a coffee.'

'Tea, please,' I said. I couldn't face any more coffee.

In the play, Claudius is always hitting the booze. Our man is very virtuous about drink-driving but he steered me upstairs to a table in yet another plastic pub and came back with sarnies and beer and my tea.

'Were you thinking of leaving the country?' he said, after a long swig.

'No,' I said.

'Where were you going, or did you intend to stay here for ever? People do, I believe. There was that guy who lived at Brussels airport for ten years . . . but he was stateless.'

I felt fairly stateless myself. Perhaps that's why I suddenly decided to tell him the truth – no, I didn't decide. I just told him.

'I bought a ticket to Dublin.'

'That's not leaving the country?'

'I was lying.'

'You do a lot of that, don't you?'

'It *was* a return.'

'Oh, good.' He started on a sandwich and seeing me look, pushed the other half across the table. 'You're not going on hunger strike?

'Now,' he said, when I'd started eating, 'there is going to be hell and the devil to pay at school. Need I say more? But do tell me, is all this on my account?'

I looked at him. He is a tall man, a bit overweight; a presence, like I said. Good–looking but pleasant with it. You couldn't imagine him being a politician, for instance. But then you couldn't imagine Shanti's Tim being a doctor.

'Yes,' I said, feeling that I'd been asked to give it to him straight, so I gave it to him straight.

'*All* of it? The truancy, the lying, the hash . . . and now this?'

'Which this?'

'Buggering off to Dublin – why Dublin for

Christ's sake?' I couldn't tell him *that*.

'We didn't think anyone would notice.'

'Of course not, you are all so quiet and unobtrusive. If you want to keep a low profile, Russell, you'd better find other friends.'

'Well, no one would have noticed – if Curt hadn't got run in.'

'You are catching my drift. Is your impending flight down to me as well?'

It was, of course. He'd paid for most of it, although I hadn't the energy to explain the complicated saga of the fifty pounds.

'It's gone,' I said. '11.45. I didn't even check in, I just went to sleep. I've hardly slept all week.'

'It shows,' Claudius said. 'You don't know what you're doing, do you?'

'I do now.'

'No, you don't. Look, for what it's worth, I don't entirely blame you. In your place I wouldn't have been over the moon, either. It couldn't have been—'

'What do you mean?'

'You know what I mean. Don't interrupt, it's hard enough to say anyway. *I* thought it was too soon.'

'Too soon?'

'To marry.'

'Why did you, then?'

He looked absolutely hopeless, helpless, knowing what he wanted to say but not getting it out.

'Don't you love her?' I said.

That gave him his cue. 'Of course I do,' he said, 'but there was you to consider.'

'But you didn't, did you?'

'Oh, I did, Russell, I did. Believe me, I did.' I could see what it cost him to say that, a kind of betrayal, but looking back I could see too that he'd wanted to say it all along, if only I'd let him. *Try not to resent me too much. I'm not trying to take your father's place . . .* he'd meant it.

He started off again. 'I thought we should wait.'

'But she didn't?'

'She wants another baby,' he said. 'And she's afraid of leaving it too late.'

There are plenty of ways of getting a baby these days that don't involve being married, that don't even involve a man, as far as I can see, but Mum has never been one to break out.

'Has that made things worse?'

'Worse than what?'

'Between us.'

'Dunno.' I didn't know. 'I always wanted another baby

173

too. Mum had a miscarriage – I suppose you knew that.'

'I'm going to get another drink,' he said. 'Are you sure you don't want one?'

'Yes, all right. I'll have what you're having.'

He came back with more sandwiches and two pints.

'What about the car?' I said.

'Oh, sod the car. I'll collect it tomorrow. We'll get the bus back. Cheers.'

We drank. The amount of alcohol I ingested in that first gulp must have been minuscule, but I got such a hit from it on my nearly-empty stomach that I felt as though I'd shot up. Not that I ever have. Not that I ever have. I seemed to be standing at some distance, in mid-air, looking back at us sitting on either side of the table, Claudius folded down into his seat, me sprawling in mine, two blokes having a pint. Very weird.

'It'll be the moment of truth on Monday,' Claudius said.

'At school? You said.'

'I had a lot of talk with Mrs Whatnot – Adam's mother – on the phone. She did most of the talking. Apparently you're all facing exclusion.'

'There was a letter.'

'I know there was a letter. There has since been

another letter. Do you want to be excluded? Quite apart from us being taken to court – or hadn't that eventuality crossed your tiny mind?'

'No.' No covered everything. I didn't want to go to school but I didn't want to be excluded. I'd known all along that Mum faced prosecution if I kept bunking off but I hadn't believed it would actually happen. That is, every time my thoughts got that far I'd terminated them, with a kind of mental humming, the way I'd hummed in Shanti's flat so I wouldn't hear what she and Adam were saying.

'Is it *that* school in particular, or any school? I mean, if we got you in somewhere else, would that help?'

'To keep me away from Adam and Curt?'

'What a lovely thought,' Claudius said. 'No, not to keep you away from Adam and Curt. Their respective parents are already contemplating steps to keep them away from you – another?'

The glasses had suddenly become empty. He didn't wait for me to answer, just got up and went over to the bar. I took out my cigarettes and lit one. When Claudius came back he looked at the packet on the table, picked it up and said, 'May I?'

'You don't smoke.'

'Neither do you.' He lit up. 'I gave up.'

'That's all I've got left.'

'Just as well. Cheers.' We drank. 'What are we going to do, Russ? I'm not going to say I don't understand you because you've worked very hard to make sure I don't understand you. But what I *really* can't understand is that theatre business.'

I couldn't think what he meant, for a moment.

'What happened? You're the last person I can imagine cutting up rough in a theatre. *Shakespeare* . . .'

'Why not?' I snarled.

'It seems to be the one thing you care about.'

'How'd you know?'

'We do live in the same house,' he said. 'Come on, what made you wreck a performance of *Hamlet*? You were really looking forward to it.'

'It wasn't me.'

'Yes it was.'

'I didn't start it. Curt—'

'Curt started it, you and Adam carried on. Like a couple of nine-year-olds.'

This is parent-speak, but he was right. That's just how we'd carried on, a bunch of nine-year-olds at a pantomime.

'I couldn't help it, I didn't want to, I knew – I thought it was disgusting even while we were doing it.

Anyway, I knew he wasn't going to.'

'Who wasn't going to what?'

'Hamlet wasn't going to kill Claudius. He spends all his time trying to find ways of not killing Claudius. Even though he knows it's his duty, he promised his father's ghost.'

'Another?' My, they were going down fast. Claudius was approaching the bar very carefully, but I was sitting at the table very carefully.

When he came back he put the glasses down equally carefully and said, 'Of course he thinks he ought to do it, but it's not the sort of thing he does.'

'Whaaaa?'

'Hamlet killing Claudius. He promises to do it because his father makes him swear to—'

'Ghost.'

'—father's ghost makes him swear to, and in the heat of the moment he thinks he's up to it, but he's not. Hamlet's an intellectual, a philosopher. When he wants to get the better of someone, he talks. When he wants to make a fool of someone, he talks. When he wants to hurt someone, he talks. When he wants to take revenge, he talks. That's what he's doing at Wittenberg, learning to win with his wits. He's not a natural-born killer. He's not even much good at it.

He only kills Polonius by accident.'

'He can fence,' I said, kind of spirited, as if I was defending an old friend who was being talked down. 'Claudius bets on him to win the contest with Laertes.'

'Only because he knows he'll lose. Even his mother says he's out of condition.'

'Why does Claudius poison the foils, then?'

'To make sure. He's good with poison, remember?'

'All goes pear-shaped though, doesn't it?'

'It all began to go pear-shaped the moment Claudius murdered his brother. Regicide . . . crime against God . . .'

It was seeping through my fuggy mind that I was talking to someone who knew the play even better than I did, but when I looked up he wasn't there.

After a few minutes he *was* there, with another round.

'You think Shakespeare meant it like that?'

'Like what?'

'Hamlet being the wrong kind of person for what he's got to do.'

'Of course he meant it. Look at the other young men in the play. Laertes is swanning around Europe, Fortinbras is leading an army – why not? Richard III was a general at eighteen, a good one. Where's Hamlet? at University reading philosophy. It's an odd thing for the King's son to be doing in those days, don't you think? Why isn't *he* leading an army? Why isn't he learning something useful?'

'It would wreck the play,' I said.

'Of course it would. If I did a production of *Hamlet* I wouldn't make him heroic. He'd be a weedy little runt with bi-focals. Now, if Hamlet were like Laertes, he wouldn't hang about thinking deeply and arguing with himself about death, he'd have had Claudius's balls on a shovel by teatime.'

'Do you know what I call you?' I said, and wished I hadn't, but it didn't seem to be me talking anyway.

Claudius stared very hard across the table at me. 'Don't tell me,' he said. His voice too came from very far away. 'Let me guess.' He took another of my cigarettes. There were only two left now. 'Polonius?'

'Why Polonius?'

'Interfering old fool.'

'Not Polonius.'

His eyes swivelled a bit while he asked himself, So who does *that* leave?

'Oh, Christ, no. Not Claudius?'

He looked appalled. I had a feeling he thought it was funny as well, but he was more appalled than amused.

'You don't think *I* killed him, do you?'

'*No.*'

'I can't take this,' he muttered, and swam away towards the bar, which seemed to be coming to meet him. While he was gone I stayed awake by watching a dried moth swinging from a single strand of cobweb, like a trapeze artist who'd died on the job and was still dangling, mummified, years later.

The light was blotted out again. A figure sitting opposite me. Two more glasses on the table.

'If I'm Claudius, what does that make Sarah? No, don't tell me, let me work it out.' He worked it out. 'Oh, *Russ.*'

'There's nobody else but Ophelia,' I said.

'Do we have an Ophelia?'

'No. She left a long time ago.'

'Not drowned?'

'Not even dead.'

'Thank God for that.' He raised his glass.

I raised mine. 'The King drinks to Hamlet.'

'Act V Scene 2. We'll all be dead in a minute.'

'Nah. No Laertes. No Horatio. Tell you what, *anyone* would have been Claudius. It's not personal.'

'Anyone who married Gertrude – Sarah?'

'Anyone who married her that fast.'

'At least it wasn't two months.'

With a shriek that could sever optic nerves, his mobe went off, and then kept on and on while we tried to find it, Claudius frisking himself while I rummaged through his overcoat. In the end we found it under the table. The shrieking stopped when he grabbed it but as he put it to his ear another shrieking started.

'Sarah, Sarah,' he kept saying. 'Sarah!'

There was a squawk.

'Sorry, yes. Yes, right away. Right now. Getting up this minute. Sorry. Yes.

'She says I'm drunk,' he said, putting the phone away.

'You are.'

'So are you.'

'So am I?'

'I said we were coming right away. I think we'd better.'

He put on his coat. I picked up the bag.

'I'll give you a hand with that,' he said, and carefully we wove our way across the crappy pub carpeting to the top of the stairs, toting the bag between us like a carry-cot and clinging to it for dear life, so when we fell down the stairs with it, we were still together at the bottom.

Another title from Hodder Children's Books

SEA HAWK, SEA MOON

Beverley Birch

She drifts. Bumping the rock. Seaweed laces her legs and her hair spreads thin on the tide. She rolls with the wave, and her face rises to look at him.

The summer Ben spends with his uncle Michael in the remote Scottish highlands is one he will never forget. Restoring his uncle's precious wreck, *Sea Hawk*, learning to sail with the mysterious Iona.

But then the dreams begin. Frightening tensions and moods surround the village. A village with secrets.

And then Iona disappears. Is this the girl of his dreams – a girl snatched by the waves, a still, dead weight beneath inhospitable crags, a girl whose misery he cannot understand?

CONTROL-SHIFT

Nick Manns

'There comes a time in every physician's career when she or he is confronted by a case so baffling, they are forced to concede that science doesn't hold the answer to all great mysteries . . .'

So begins a tale that leads to some of the most sensational evidence ever to grace the stage of an English law court. In their new home in an old country house, Graham's father designs a computer-guided, state-of-the-art weapons system.

But Graham and his sistery Matty sense they are not alone in the house. Bleak and terrifying secrets hover – secrets that will shift the very foundation of their lives . . .

SEED TIME

Nick Manns

To begin with he couldn't make anything out in the shadows thrown by the trees, but then he saw a black shape take form in the grey . . .

It was Michael's idea – excluded from school and reckless since the loss of his father. They cycled to the heath on a Friday. Tony played truant, lying to his parents – trying not to think of their faces already stretched taut by threatening financial ruin.

Michael drew it from the water – a long-buried treasure dripping slime and algae. And with it came new conflicts, new hopes and new ways of thinking for the boys, their families and their community . . .

STUCK IN NEUTRAL

Terry Trueman

My life is one of those 'good news – bad news' jokes. I could go on about my good news for hours, but you probably want to hear the punch line, my bad news, right? First off, my parents got divorced ten years ago because of me. My dad didn't divorce my mother, or my sister, Cindy, or my brother, Paul – he divorced me. He couldn't handle my condition, so he had to leave. My condition? Well, that brings us to the guts of my bad news.

Shawn has severe cerebral palsy. No control over his muscles, no means of communication – no hope of improvement. Yet humour, joy and love sit alongside frustration in Shawn's mind. Physically powerless, his internal life is full of pleasure.

Shawn's father perceives only pain, waste, the devastation of an uninhabited body. And as his father's sorrow builds, Shawn suspects that so does his desire to act . . .